RALPH THE TRAIN DISPATCHER

BY

ALLEN CHAPMAN

Ralph The Train Dispatcher

CHAPTER I—THE OVERLAND EXPRESS

"Those men will bear watching--they are up to some mischief, Fairbanks."

"I thought so myself, Mr. Fogg. I have been watching them for some time."

"I thought you would notice them--you generally do notice things."

The speaker with these words bestowed a glance of genuine pride and approbation upon his companion, Ralph Fairbanks.

They were a great pair, these two, a friendly, loyal pair, the grizzled old veteran fireman, Lemuel Fogg, and the clear-eyed, steady-handed young fellow who had risen from roundhouse wiper to switchtower service, then to fireman, then to engineer, and who now pulled the lever on the crack racer of the Great Northern Railroad, the Overland express.

Ralph sat with his hand on the throttle waiting for the signal to pull out of Boydsville Tracks. Ahead were clear, as he well knew, and his eyes were fixed on three men who had just passed down the platform with a scrutinizing glance at the locomotive and its crew.

Fogg had watched them for some few minutes with an ominous eye. He had snorted in his characteristic, suspicious way, as the trio lounged around the end of the little depot.

"Good day," he now said with fine sarcasm in his tone, "hope I see you again--know I'll see you again. They're up to tricks, Fairbanks, and don't you forget it."

"Gone, have they?" piped in a new voice, and a brakeman craned his neck from his position on the reverse step of the locomotive. "Say, who are they, anyway?"

"Do you know?" inquired the fireman, facing the intruder sharply.

"I'd like to. They got on three stations back. The conductor spotted them as odd fish from the start. Two of them are disguised, that's sure--the mustache of one of them went sideways. The old man, the mild-looking, placid old gentleman they had in tow, is a telegrapher."

"How do you know that?" asked Ralph, becoming interested.

"That's easy. I caught him strumming on the car window sill, and I have had an apprenticeship in the wire line long enough to guess what he was tapping out. On his mind, see--force of habit and all that. The two with him, though, looked like jail birds."

"What struck me," interposed Fogg, "was the way they snooked around the train at the two last stops. They looked us over as if they were planning a holdup."

"Yes, and they pumped the train hands dry all about your schedule," declared the brakeman. "Cottoned to me, but I cut them short. Seemed mightily interested in the pay car routine, by the way."

"Did, eh," bristled up Fogg. "Say, tell us about that."

"Why, you see--There goes the starting signal. See you again."

The brakeman dropped back to duty, and the depot and the three men who had caused a brief ripple in the monotony of a routine run were lost in the distance. For a few minutes the fireman had his hands full feeding the fire, and Ralph, eyes, ears and all his senses on the alert, got in perfect touch with throttle, air gauge and exhaust valve.

Ralph glanced at the clock and took an easy position on his cushioned seat. Everything was in order for a smooth run to twenty miles away. The Overland Express was on time, as she usually was, and everything was in trim for a safe delivery at terminus.

Fogg hustled about. He was a restless, ambitious being, always finding lots to do about cab and tender. His brows were knitted, however, and every once in a while he indulged in a fit of undertoned grumbling. Ralph watched him furtively with a slight smile. He knew that his companion railroader was stirred up about something. The young engineer had come to understand the quirks and turns and moods of his eccentric helper, just as fully as those of his beloved engine.

"I say," broke out Fogg finally, slamming down into his seat. "It's about time for something to happen, Fairbanks."

"Think so?" queried Ralph lightly.

"Been pretty smooth sailing lately, you see."

"That's the way it ought to be in a well-regulated family, isn't it, Mr. Fogg?"

"Humph--maybe. All the same, I'm an old bird and know the signs."

"What signs are you talking about, Mr. Fogg?"

"Our machine balked this morning when she took the turntable, didn't she?"

"That was because the wiper was half asleep."

"Thirteen blew out a cylinder head as we passed her--13, an unlucky number, see?"

"That's an every-day occurrence since the high pressure system came in."

"White cow crossed the track just back a bit."

"Nonsense," railed Ralph. "I thought you'd got rid of all those old superstitions since your promotion to the best job on the road."

"That's it, that's just it," declared the fireman with serious vehemence--"and I don't want to lose it. Just as I say, since we knocked out the sorehead crew of strikers and made the big record on that famous snowstorm run on the Mountain Division, we've been like ducks in clear water, smooth sailing and the best on earth none too good for us. It isn't natural. Why, old John Griscom, thirty years at the furnace, used to get scared to death if he ran two weeks without a broken driving wheel or a derail."

"Well, you see we're on a new order of things, Mr. Fogg," suggested Ralph brightly. "They've put us at the top-notch with a top-notch machine and a top-notch crew. We must stay there, and we'll do it if we keep our heads clear, eyes open and attend strictly to business."

The fireman shook his head fretfully and looked unconvinced. Ralph knew his stubborn ways and said nothing.

The young engineer of the Overland Express was in the heyday of satisfaction and contentment. He was proud of his present position, and was prouder still because he felt that he had earned it through sheer energy and merit. As Fogg had declared, the appearance of the three men noted had something sinister about it, but the fireman was always getting rattled about something or other, fussy as an old woman when the locomotive was balky. Ralph insisted upon enjoying to the limit the full measure of prosperity that had come to him.

Both had fought hard to secure the positions they now held, however, and the mere hint of a break in the pleasant programme set them up in arms instanter. They had chummed together and had learned to love the staunch, magnificent locomotive that pulled the Overland Express as if it was a fellow comrade, and would have had a pitched battle any time with the meddler or enemy who plotted injury to the prize train of the Great Northern.

All this had not been accomplished without some pretty hard knocks. Looking back in retrospect now, Ralph could fancy his progress to date as veritable steps in the ladder of fortune. It had all rounded out so beautifully that it seemed like a dream. Now the thought of trouble or disaster reminded him gravely of the foes he had known in the past, and the difficult places he had battled through in his steadfast march to the front rank.

Ralph Fairbanks had taken to railroading as naturally as does a duck to water. His father had been one of the pioneer builders of the Great Northern. In the first volume of the present series, entitled "Ralph of the Roundhouse," the unworthy scheme of Gasper Farrington, a village magnate, to rob

Ralph's widowed mother of her little home was depicted. That book, too, tells of how Ralph left school to work for a living and win laurels as the best engine wiper in the service.

Ralph's next step up the ladder, as told in the second volume of this series, called "Ralph in the Switch Tower," led to his promotion to the post of fireman. The third volume of the series, "Ralph on the Engine," showed the routine and adventures of an ambitious boy bound to reach the top notch in railroad service.

The proudest moment in the life of the young engineer, however, seemed to have arrived when Ralph was awarded the crack run of the road, as told in the fourth volume of this series entitled "Ralph on the Overland Express."

The reader who has followed the upward and onward course of the railroad boy through these volumes will remember how he made friends everywhere. They were all the better for his bright ways and good example. It was Ralph's great forbearance and patience that overcame the grumpiness and suspicion of the cross-grained Lemuel Fogg and made of him a first-class fireman. It was Ralph's kindly encouragement that brought out the inventive genius of a capital young fellow named Archie Graham, and helped Limpy Joe, a railroad cripple, to acquire a living as an eating house proprietor.

A poor waif named Van Sherwin owed his rise in life to the influence of the good-hearted young engineer, and Zeph Dallas, a would-be boy detective, was toned down and instructed by Ralph until his wild ideas had some practical coherency to them.

Ralph had his enemies. From time to time along his brisk railroad career they had bobbed up at inopportune junctures, but never to his final disaster, for they were in the wrong and right always prevails in the end. They had tried to upset his plans on many an occasion, they had tried to disgrace and discredit him, but vainly.

In "Ralph on the Overland Express" the young engineer did some pretty big things for a new man at the throttle. He carried a train load of passengers through a snowstorm experience that made old veterans on the road take notice in an astonished way, and he made some record runs over the Mountain Division that established the service of the Great Northern as a standard model.

All this success not only ranked in the minds of his enemies, but roused the envy and dissatisfaction of rival roads. For some time vague hints had been rife that these rivals were forming a combination "to put the Great Northern out of business," if the feat were possible, so both Ralph and his loyal fireman kept their eyes wide open and felt that they were on their mettle all of the time.

Ralph's last exploit had won him a high place in the estimation of his superiors. With every train out of Rockton stalled, he and Fogg had made a terrifying hairbreadth special run to Shelby Junction, defying floods, drifts and washouts, landing the president of the road just in the nick of time to catch a train on a parallel rival line.

The event had enabled that official to close an advantageous arrangement, in which time was the essence of a contract which gave the Great Northern the supremacy over every line in the district having transcontinental connections.

The Great Northern had won the upper hand through this timely but not tricky operation. Naturally, baffled, rival roads had been upset by the same. A revengeful feeling had extended to the employees of those lines, and the warning had been spread broadcast to look out for squalls, as the other roads had given the quiet tip to its men, it was understood, to take down the Great Northern a peg or two whenever occasion offered.

Of all this Ralph was thinking as they passed the flag station at Luce, and shot around the long curve guarded by a line of bluffs just beyond. The young engineer was thinking of home, and so was Fogg, for they were due in twenty-three minutes now.

Suddenly Ralph reached out for the lever lightning quick, and then his hand swept sand and air valves with the rapidity of an expert playing some instrument.

Crack!

Under the wheels of the big locomotive a detonating clamor rang out--always a vivid warning to the nerves of every wide-awake railroad man.

"A torpedo--something ahead," spoke Ralph quickly.

"What did I tell you?" jerked out his fireman excitedly. "I felt it in my bones, I told you it was about time for something to happen."

The young engineer steadied the locomotive down to a sliding halt like a trained jockey stopping a horse on the race track. The halt brought the nose of the locomotive just beyond the bluff line so that Ralph could sweep the tracks ahead with a clear glance.

"It's a wreck," announced the young engineer of the Overland Express.

CHAPTER II—THE WRECK

"A wreck, eh,--sure, I know it! Our turn next--you'll see," fumed Fogg, as the locomotive came to a stop.

"It's a freight on the out track," said Ralph, peering ahead. "Two cars over the embankment and--"

"For land's sake!" interrupted the fireman, "whiff! whoo! what have we run into, anyway?"

A flying object came slam bang against the lookout window not two inches from Fogg's nose. A dozen more sailed over the cab roof. With a great flutter half of these dropped down into the cab direct.

"Chickens!" roared Fogg in excitement and astonishment. "Say, did you ever see so many at one time? Where do they ever come from?"

"From the wreck. Look ahead," directed Ralph.

It was hard to do this, for a second flock of fowls thronged down upon them. Of a sudden there seemed to be chickens everywhere. They scampered down the rails, crouched to the pilot, roosted on the steam chests, lined up on the coal of the tender, while three fat hens clucked and skirmished under the very feet of the fireman, who was hopping about to evade the bewildering inrush.

"I declare!" he ejaculated breathlessly.

Far as Ralph could see ahead, stray fowls were in evidence. Feathers were flying, and a tremendous clatter and bustle was going on. They came limping, flying, rolling along the roadbed from the direction of a train standing stationary on the out track. In its center there was a gap. Thirty feet down the embankment, split in two, and a mere pile of kindling wood now, were two cars.

The trucks of one of these and some minor wreckage littered the in track. Freight hands were clearing it away, and it was this temporary obstruction that had been the cause of the warning torpedo.

A brakeman from the freight came to the passenger train to report what was doing.

"Palace chicken car and a gondola loaded with boxes in the ditch beyond," he said. "We'll be cleaned up for you in a few minutes."

"That's how the chickens come to be in evidence so numerously, it seems," remarked Ralph.

"Say, see them among the wrecked wire netting, and putting for the timber!" exclaimed Fogg. "Fairbanks, there's enough poultry running loose to stock an eating house for a year. I say, they're nobody's property now. Suppose--here's two fat ones. I reckon I'll take that much of the spoil while it's going."

With a vast chuckle the fireman grabbed two of the fowls under his feet and dumped them into his waste box, shutting down the cover. The conductor of the freight came up penciling a brief report. He handed it to the conductor of the Overland.

"We'll wire from Luce," he explained, "but we may be delayed reaching there and you may get this to headquarters at the Junction first. Tell the claim agent there won't be salvage enough to fill a waybill. She's clear," with a glance down the track.

The Overland proceeded slowly past the wreck, affording the crew and the curious passengers a view of the demolished freight lying at the bottom of the embankment. Once past this, Ralph set full steam to make up for lost time.

It put Fogg in better humor to arrive on schedule. The thought of home comforts close by and the captured chickens occupied his mind and dissipated his superstitious forebodings.

When they reached the roundhouse the fireman started straight for home. Ralph lingered a few minutes to chat with the foreman, and was about to leave when Fry, the claim agent of the road, came into the doghouse in great haste.

"Just the man I want to see, Fairbanks," he said animatedly.

"That so?" smiled Ralph.

"Yes. Your conductor just notified me of the smashup beyond the limits. It looks clean cut enough, with the tracks cleared, but he says some of the stuff is perishable."

"If you list chickens in that class," responded Ralph, "I guess that's right."

"That's the bother of it," observed Fry. "Dead salvage could wait, and the wrecking crew could take care of it at their leisure, but--live stock!"

"It looked to me as if most of the chickens had got away," exclaimed Ralph. "The car was split and twisted from end to end."

"I reckon I had better get on the job instanter," said the claim agent. "How about getting down to the bluff switch, Forgan?"

"Nothing moving but the regulars," reported the roundhouse foreman. "You don't need a special?"

"No, any dinky old machine will do."

"Gravel pit dummy just came in."

"Can't you rig her up and give me clear tracks for an hour, till I make investigations?"

"Crew gone home."

"No extras on hand?"

The foreman consulted his schedule and shook his head negatively.

Ralph thought of his home and mother, but a certain appealing glance from the claim agent and a natural disposition to be useful and accommodating influenced him to a kindly impulse.

"See here, Mr. Fry, I'll be glad to help you out, if I can," he said.

"You certainly can, Fairbanks, and I won't forget the favor," declared the claim agent warmly. "You see, I'm booked for a week's vacation and a visit to my old invalid father down at Danley, beginning tomorrow. If I can untie all the red tape from this wreck affair, I'm free to get out, and my substitute can take up any fresh tangles that come up tomorrow."

"Can you fire?" inquired Ralph.

"I can make a try at it."

"Then I'll see to the rest," promised the young engineer briskly.

With the aid of wiper Ralph soon got the dummy ready for action. It was a long time since the young engineer had done roundhouse duty. He did it well now, and thanked the strict training of his early apprentice experience. The jerky spiteful little engine rolled over the turntable in a few minutes time, and the claim agent pulled off his coat and looked to Ralph for orders.

They took a switch and headed down the clear out track. At a crossing a man came tearing towards them, arms waving, long beard flying, and his face showing the greatest urgency and excitement.

"Mishter Fry! Mishter Fry!" he panted out, "I haf just heard--"

"Nothing for you, Cohen," shouted the claim agent.

"I hear dere vas some boxes. Sthop! sthop! I've got the retty gash."

"Ready-Cash Cohen," exclaimed Fry to Ralph. "Always on hand when there's any cheap wreck salvage lying around loose. That fellow seems to scent a wreck like a vulture."

"I've heard of him," remarked Ralph with a smile.

They had free swing on the out track until they neared the scene of the wreck. Here they took a siding and left the dummy, to walk to the spot where the two freight cars had gone over the embankment.

"Hello!" suddenly ejaculated the claim agent with tremendous surprise and emphasis.

"Excuse me, Mishter Fry, but that salvage--"

Ralph burst out into a hearty peal of laughter. Clinging to the little bobtail tender of the dummy was Ready-Cash Cohen.

"Well, you're a good one, Cohen."

"If I vas'nt, vould I be Chonny-on-de-spot, Mishter Fry?" chuckled Cohen cunningly.

He followed them as they walked down the tracks. When they reached the point where the two freights had gone over the embankment, Fry clambered down its slant and for some time poked about the tangled mass of wreckage below.

"Vill dere haf to be an appraisal, my tear friend?" anxiously inquired Cohen, pressing forward as the claim agent reappeared.

"No," responded Fry shortly. "There's a chicken car with live and dead mixed up in the tangle. Come, Cohen, how much for the lot?"

"Schickens?" repeated Cohen disgustedly--"not in my line, Mishter Fry. Schickens are an expense. Dey need feeding."

"Won't bid, eh?"

"Don't vant dem at any price. But de boxes, Mishter Fry--vot's in dose boxes?"

"See here," observed Fry, "I'm not giving information to the enemy. There they are, badly shaken up but they look meaty, don't they? If you want to bid unsight unseen, name your figure."

"Fifty tollars."

"Take them."

The salvage dealer toppled down the embankment with a greedy promptness. The claim agent winked blandly after him.

"I expected it," said Fry, as a minute later Cohen came toiling up the embankment his face a void of disappointed misery.

"Mishter Fry, Mishter Fry," he gasped, "dey are looking glasses!"

"Found that out, did you?" grinned the freight agent.

"Dey vos smashed, dey vas proken, every last one of dem. Dey are not even junk. My tear friend, I cannot take dem."

"A bargain's a bargain, Cohen," voiced Fry smoothly. "You've made enough out of your deals with the road to stand by your bid. If you don't, we're no longer your customer."

"I von't have dem. It was a trick," and the man went down the track tearing at his beard.

"There's kindling wood there for somebody free for the taking," remarked Fry. "The chicken smashup isn't so easy."

"Many down there?" inquired Ralph.

"Yes, most of them are crushed, but a good many alive are shut in the wire tangle. The best I can do is to send a section man to pry them free. It's heartless to leave them to suffer and to die."

"A lot of them got free," observed Ralph.

"They're somewhere around the diggings. It wouldn't be a bad speculation for some bright genius to round them up. Why, say, Fairbanks, you're an ambitious kind of a fellow. I'll offer you an investment."

"What's that, Mr. Fry?" inquired the young engineer.

"I'll sell you the whole kit and caboodle in the car and out of it for twenty-five dollars."

Ralph shook his head with a smile.

"If I had time to spare I'd jump at your offer, Mr. Fry," he said. "As it is, what could I do with the proposition?"

"Do?" retorted the claim agent. "Hire some boys to gather in the bunch. There may be five hundred chicks in the round up."

"Really, I couldn't bother with it, Mr. Fry," began Ralph, and then he turned abruptly.

Some one had pulled at his sleeve, and with a start the young engineer stared strangely at a boy about his own age.

CHAPTER III—TROUBLE BREWING

The strange boy appeared upon the scene so suddenly that Ralph decided he must have reached the roadbed from the other side of the embankment.

The young engineer faced him with a slight start. To his certain knowledge he had never seen the lad before. However, his face so strongly resembled that of some one he had met recently it puzzled Ralph. Whom did those features suggest? Ralph thought hard, but gave it up.

"Did you wish to see me?" he inquired.

The boy had a striking face. It was pale and thin, his clothes were neat but shabby. There was a sort of scared look in his eyes that appealed to Ralph, who was strongly sympathetic.

"I know you," spoke the boy in a hesitating, embarrassed way. "You don't know me, but I've had you pointed out to me."

"That so?" and Ralph smiled.

"You are Ralph Fairbanks, the engineer of the Overland Express," continued the lad in a hushed tone, as if the distinction awed him.

"That's right," nodded Ralph.

"Well, I've heard of you, and you've been a friend to a good many people. I hope I'm not over bold, but if you would be a friend to me--"

Here the strange boy paused in a pitiful, longing way that appealed to Ralph.

"Go ahead," he said.

"I heard this gentleman," indicating Mr. Fry, "offer to sell the chickens down the embankment. I'm a poor boy, Mr. Fairbanks--dreadfully poor. There's reasons why I can't work in the towns like other boys. You can give me work, though--you can just set me on my feet."

"How can I do that?" inquired Ralph, getting interested.

"By buying me those chickens. I've got the place for them, I've got the time to attend to them, and I know just how to handle them. Why," continued the speaker excitedly, "there's nearly two hundred in prime trim gathered in a little thicket over yonder, and there's double that number among the wreckage, besides those that are hurt that I can nurse and mend up. If you will buy them for me, I'll solemnly promise to return you the money in a week and double the amount of interest in two."

"You talk clear and straight and earnest, my lad," here broke in the claim agent. "What's your name?"

"Glen Palmer."

"Do you live near here?"

"Yes, sir--in an old abandoned farmhouse, rent free, about a mile north of here."

"With your folks?"

"No, sir, I have no folks, only an old grandfather. He's past working, and, well, a--a little queer at times, and I have to keep close watch of him. That's what's the trouble."

The claim agent took out his note book.

"Look here," he spoke, "if Fairbanks will vouch for you, I'll tab off the chickens to you at fifteen dollars, due in thirty days."

"O--oh!" gasped the lad, clasping his hands in an ecstacy of hope and happiness. "I'll be sure to pay you-- Why, with what I know I can do with those chickens, I could pay you ten times over inside of a month."

"Mr. Fry," said Ralph, studying the boy's face for a moment or two, "I'll go security for my friend here."

"Say--excuse me, but say, Mr. Fairbanks, I--I--"

The boy broke down, tears chocking his utterance. He could only clasp and cling to Ralph's hand. The latter patted him on the shoulder with the encouraging words:

"You go ahead with your chicken farm, Glen, and if it needs more capital come to me."

"If you only knew what you've done for me--for me and my old grandfather!" faltered Glen Palmer, the deepest gratitude and feeling manifested in tone and manner.

Ralph felt sure that the lad had a history. He did not, however, embarrass him with any questioning. He liked the way that young Palmer talked and bustled about as soon as the word was given that his proposition was accepted. With an eager face he announced that he had a plan for getting the chickens to his home, and darted off at breakneck speed, waving his hand gratefully back at Ralph a dozen times.

Ralph and the claim agent reached the dummy to find Cohen hanging around it in great mental distress. Fry invited him to ride in the cab, and tormented him by talking about his bargain clear back to the roundhouse. Then he relieved Cohen's distress, which bordered on positive distraction, by releasing him from his contract.

Mrs. Fairbanks greeted Ralph with her usual loving, kindly welcome when he reached home. The old family cottage was a veritable nest of comfort, and the young engineer enjoyed it to the utmost. There was always some special favorite dainty awaiting Ralph on his return from a trip, and he had a fine appetizing meal.

"We had a visitor today, Ralph," said Mrs. Fairbanks, as they sat chatting in the cozy sitting room a little later.

"Who was that, mother?"

Mrs. Fairbanks with a smile handed her son a card that had been lying on the mantle. Ralph smiled, too, as he looked it over.

"H'm," he said. "Quite dignified, 'Mr. Dallas,' our old friend Zeph, eh? What's this mysterious monogram, cryptogram, or whatever it is, way down in the corner of the card?"

"It looks like two S's," suggested Mrs. Fairbanks.

"Oh, I can solve the enigma now," said Ralph with a broader smile than ever. "It is 'S. S.,' by which Zeph means and wants mystified others to half guess means 'Secret Service.' There's one thing about Zeph, with all his wild imaginings and ambition along the railroad line, he sticks to his idea of breaking in somewhere as an active young sleuth."

"We think a lot of Zeph, Ralph, and we mustn't forget that he did some bright things in helping that poor little orphan, Ernest Gregg, to health and happiness."

"Yes, Zeph deserves great credit for his patience and cleverness in that affair," admitted Ralph warmly, "only the line he is so fascinated with doesn't strike me as a regular business."

"How about Mr. Adair, Ralph?" insinuated his mother.

"That's so, Bob Adair is the finest railroad detective in the world. If Zeph could line up under his guidance, he might make something practical of himself."

"I think he has really done just that."

"I am delighted to hear it," said Ralph, and watching the glowing embers in the grate in a dreamy fashion he mused pleasantly over his experience with the redoubtable Zeph, while his mother was busy tidying up the dining room.

It was a good deal of satisfaction for Ralph to recall Zeph Dallas to mind. Zeph, a raw country youth, had come to Stanley Junction in a whole peck of trouble. Ralph had always a helping hand for the unlucky or unfortunate. He became a good friend to Zeph and got him a place in the roundhouse. Zeph made a miserable failure of the job. The height of his ambition was to be a detective--like fellows he had read about.

Zeph finally landed, as he expressed it, with both feet. The son of a prominent railroad official became interested in hunting up the relatives of a forlorn little fellow named Gregg. He had plenty of money, and he hired Zeph to assist him. The latter showed that he had something in him, for his wit and energy not only located the wealthy relative of the orphan outcast, but upset the plots of a wicked schemer who was planning to rob the friendless lad of his rights.

"What did Zeph say about Mr. Adair, mother?" inquired Ralph, as Mrs. Fairbanks again entered the sitting room.

"Nothing clear," she explained. "You know how Zeph delights in cuddling up his ideas to himself and looking and acting mysterious. He was very important as he hinted that Mr. Adair depended on him to 'save the day in a big case,' and he said a great deal about a 'rival railroad.'"

"Oh, did he, indeed?" murmured Ralph thoughtfully.

"Zeph told me to advise you, very secretly he put it, to look out for trouble."

"What kind of trouble?"

"Particularly, he said, in the train dispatcher's department."

"Hm!" commented the young engineer simply, but his brow became furrowed with thought, and he reflected by spells quite seriously over the subject during the evening.

Fogg had forgotten all about his fears of the day previous when he reported at the roundhouse the next morning. He grinned at his young comrade with a particularly satisfied smirk on his face, and made the remark:

"You see before you, young man, a person full of the best chicken stew ever cooked in Stanley Junction. I say, Fairbanks, if you'd kind of slow up going past Bluff Point we might grab off enough more of those chickens to do for Sunday dinner."

"We? Don't include me in your disreputable pilferings, Mr. Fogg," declared Ralph, "you may get a bill for the two fowls you so boastingly allude to."

"Hey."

"Yes, indeed. In fact," continued Ralph with mock seriousness, "I don't know but what I may have a certain interest in enforcing its collection."

The young engineer recited the episode of the salvage sale of the chickens to Glen Palmer.

"Quite a windfall, that," commented Fogg. "Another fellow to thank his lucky stars that he ran up against Ralph Fairbanks. Sort of interested in this proposition myself. I can hardly imagine a finer prospect than running a chicken farm. Some day--"

The rhapsody of Fireman Fogg was cut short by the arrival of the schedule minute for getting up steam on the Overland racer. The bustle and energy of starting out on their regular trip made engineer and helper forget everything except the duties of the occasion. As they cleared the limits, however, and approached Bluff Point, Ralph watched out with natural curiosity, and Fogg remarked:

"Hope a few more chickens drop into the cab this morning."

Ralph slowed up slightly, they struck the bluff curve, and as they neared the scene of the freight wreck of the previous day he had a good view of the embankment where the two abandoned cars lay.

"Some one there," commented Fogg, his keen glance fixed on the spot.

"Yes, our young friend Glen Palmer and an old man. That must be the grandfather he talked about. They are very industriously at work."

The two persons whom Ralph designated were in the midst of the wreckage. The old man was prying apart the netted compartment of the car and into this the boy was reaching. Near at hand was an old hand cart. It carried a great coop made of laths, and was half filled with fowls.

As the train circled the spot the boy below suspended his work and looked up. He seemed to recognize Ralph--or at least he knew his locomotive.

Ralph nodded and smiled and sounded three quick low toots from the whistle. This attracted the attention of the old man, who, standing upright, stared up at the train, posed like some heroic figure in plain view.

"I say!" ejaculated Fogg with a great start.

The young engineer was similarly moved. In a flash he now traced the source of the puzzling suggestiveness of something familiar in the face of Glen Palmer the day before.

"Did you see him?" demanded Fogg.

"Yes," nodded Ralph.

"The old man--he's the one we saw with those two suspicious jailbird-looking fellows down the line yesterday."

CHAPTER IV—THE WIRE TAPPERS

"I don't like it," spoke Fogg with emphasis.

"Neither do I," concurred Ralph, "but I fancy the sensible thing to do is to make the best of it."

"While somebody else is making the worst of it!" grumbled the old fireman. "What brought up the confab with the old man at the terminus, anyway?"

"He just called me into the office and gave me the warning I have told you about."

"Queer--and pestiferous," said Fogg with vehemence. "I don't mind a fair and square fight with any man, but this stabbing in the back, tumbling into man traps in the dark and the like, roils me."

The Overland Express was on its return trip to Stanley Junction. Outside of the incident of the recognition of the old grandfather of Glen Palmer at the bluff curve, nothing had occurred to disturb a smooth, satisfactory run. Ralph and Fogg had discussed the first incident for quite some time after it had come up.

"I don't like the lineup," Fogg had asserted. "Here one day you run across that old man in the company of two fellows we'd put in jail on mere suspicion. The next day we find the same old man cleaning up a wreck. Is that part of some villanious programme? Did some fine play send that chicken car down into the ditch, say?"

"Decidedly not," answered Ralph. "It doesn't look that way at all. Even if it did, I would vouch for young Palmer. He had no hand in it. I'll look this business up, though, when we get back home."

"H'm, you'd better," growled Fogg, and the fireman was back in his old surly suspicious mood all of the rest of the run.

Now, on the return trip, Fogg was brought up to a positive pitch of frenzy. It was just after their layover at Rockton when a messenger had come from the assistant superintendent to the roundhouse. The waiting hands there knew him. He approached Ralph, addressed him in a low confidential tone, and the two proceeded to headquarters together. It was the sentiment of the majority that the young engineer of the Overland Express was "on the carpet for a call down."

Ralph came back from the interview with the railway official with a serious but by no means downcast face. He parried the good natured raillery of his fellow workmen. It was not until he and his fireman were well out of Rockton on their return trip that he told Fogg what had taken place in the private office of the assistant superintendent.

There was not much to tell, but there was lots left to surmise, and worry over, according to Fogg's way of thinking. The railroad official had pledged Ralph to treat the interview as strictly confidential, except so far as his fireman was concerned. There was trouble brewing unmistakably, he told Ralph. The latter had weathered some pretty hard experiences with personal enemies and strikers in the past. The official wished to prepare him to battle some more of it in the future.

Bluntly he informed Ralph that two rival roads were "after the scalp" of the Great Northern. They could not reach the Overland schedule of the latter line by fair means, and they might try to break it by foul ones. The official gravely announced that he felt sure of this. He would have later specific information for Ralph. In the meantime, he wished him to exercise unusual vigilance and efficiency in overcoming obstacles that might arise to delay or cripple the Overland Express.

Two things rather startled the young engineer, for they seemed to confirm hints and suspicions already in the wind. In a guarded way the official had referred to "harmony in the train dispatcher's office." He had next made an allusion to the fact that if competitive rivalry grew fierce, it might attract under cover a lot of disreputable criminals, and he spoke of extra precaution when the pay trips of the line were made, tallying precisely with suspicions already entertained by Ralph.

It was a very cold night when the train started out on its return trip. It was clear starlight, however, and once on the free swing down the glistening rails, the exhilarating swirl of progress drove away all shadows of care and fear. The magnificent locomotive did her duty well and puffed down to the regular stop beyond The Barrens an hour after daylight fresh as a daisy, and just as pretty as one, Fogg declared.

"They're going to miss us this time, I reckon," spoke the fireman with hilarity and relief, as they later covered the first fifty miles beyond the Mountain Division.

"If any one was laying for us, yes, it seems so," joined in Ralph. "We are pretty well on our way, it's daytime, and likely we'll get through safe this trip."

Both were congratulating themselves on the outlook as they struck the first series of curves that led through the long stretch of bluffs at the end of which they had encountered the torpedo warning just seventy-two hours previous. There was no indication of any obstruction ahead, and the locomotive was going at good speed.

It was almost a zigzag progress on a six per cent. grade for a stretch of over ten miles, and five of the distance it was a blind swift whiz, shut in by great towering bluffs without a break.

Suddenly at a sharp turn Fogg uttered a shout and Ralph grasped the lever with a quick clutch.

"What was that?" gasped Fogg.

"Maybe a flying rock," suggested Ralph. He spoke calmly enough, but every nerve was on the jump. The crisis of the vigilance since the run commenced had reached its climax of excitement and strain.

"Something busted," added Fogg a trifle hoarsely, "something struck the headlight and splintered it. See here," and he picked up and showed to Ralph a splinter of glass that had blown in through the open window on his side of the cab.

"Whatever it was it's past now and no damage done," declared Ralph. "There's something twisted around the steam chest, Mr. Fogg."

"So there is," assented Fogg, peering ahead. "Guess I'll see what it means."

Ralph did not have to let down speed to accommodate his expert helper. Fogg was as much at home on the running board with the train going a mile a minute pace as a house painter on a first-floor scaffold. He crept out through his window.

Ralph lost sight of him beyond the bulge of the boiler and while watching ahead from his own side of the cab. Fogg was nearly three minutes on his tour of investigation.

"There's something to think about," he declared emphatically as he dropped two objects on the floor of the cab.

"What is it?" inquired Ralph with a curious stare.

"Wait till I mend the fire and I'll show you something," said the fireman. Then, this duty attended to, he took from the floor a long piece of wire wound around a part of a device that resembled a telegraph instrument.

"See here," explained the fireman excitedly, "I've got it in a word."

"And what is that, Mr. Fogg?"

"Wire tappers."

"Or line repairers," suggested Ralph.

"I said wire tappers," insisted Fogg convincedly, "and I stick to it. They were at work back there in the cut. Their line must have sagged where they strung it too low. Our smokestack struck it, whipped the outfit free, stand and all, and that metal jigger there swung around and struck the headlight."

"What stand--was there a stand, then?" inquired Ralph.

"Must have been, for pieces of it are out on the pilot. Say, something else, too! The whole business came that way. Look at that."

Fogg lifted a small strap satchel from the floor of the cab as he spoke. This was pretty well riddled. In the general swing of the outfit its side must have come in contact with some sharp edged projection of the locomotive. Then, one side torn open from which there protruded some article of wearing apparel, it had landed on the pilot where Fogg had found it.

"Line repairers do not carry little dinky reticules like that," scornfully declaimed the fireman. "There's a dress shirt, a fancy vest and a pair of kid gloves in it. The old man at terminus was right. Some one is trying to do up the Great Northern."

"Put these things away carefully," directed Ralph, his face thoughtful, and as they ran on it grew anxious and serious.

When they passed the scene of the freight wreck three days previous, they found the debris cleared away and no sign of the boy and old man who had interested them. A wrecking crew had men at work and only a litter of kindling wood marked the scene of the tumble down the embankment.

When they reached their destination Ralph made a package of the articles Fogg had found on the pilot and proceeded to the office of the general superintendent. That functuary he found to be absent. He followed the promptings of his own mind and proceeded to the office of the road detective, Bob Adair.

A bright young fellow named Dayton, the stenographer of the road detective, announced that Mr. Adair was off duty away from Stanley Junction.

"How soon can you reach him?" inquired Ralph.

"Oh, that's easy," replied Dayton.

Adair was a warm friend of Ralph. The latter knew the official reposed a good deal of confidence in young Dayton. He decided to tell him about the supposed discovery of the wire tapping outfit.

"Good for you," commended Dayton. "You've hit a subject of big importance just at present, Mr. Fairbanks."

"Is that so."

"Very much so. I'll get word to Mr. Adair at once. He happens to be in call this side of the Mountain Division. This discovery of yours fits in--that is, Mr. Adair will be glad to get this bit of news."

"I understand," returned Ralph meaningly. He was a trifle surprised to see Dayton begin a message in cypher to his chief.

"It looks as if Mr. Adair doesn't even trust the wires just now," soliloquized Ralph as he started for home.

The first thing he did after supper was to undo the parcel containing the telegraphic device and the satchel.

The latter, as Fogg had stated, contained a shirt, a fancy vest and a pair of gloves. These bore no initial or other marks of identification. They were pretty badly riddled from their forcible collision with some sharp corner of the locomotive--so much so, that a pocket, ripped clear out of place, revealed a folded slip of paper. This had suffered in the mix-up, like the garments. Ralph opened it carefully.

It was tattered and torn, sections were gouged out of it here and there, but Ralph devoted to its perusal a thorough inspection.

His face was both startled and thoughtful as he looked up from his desk. For nearly five minutes the young railroader sat staring into space, his mind wrestling with a mighty problem.

Ralph arose from his chair at last, put on his cap and went to the kitchen where Mrs. Fairbanks was tidying up things.

"I'm going away for an hour or two, mother," he announced.

"Nothing wrong, I hope, Ralph," spoke Mrs. Fairbanks, the serious manner of her son arousing her mothering anxiety at once.

"I don't know," answered Ralph. "It's something pretty important. I've got to see the paymaster of the road."

CHAPTER V—IKE SLUMP

"Things are narrowing down and closing in," said the young engineer to himself as he left the Fairbanks cottage.

Ralph started away at a brisk pace. As he had told his mother, he was anxious to see the paymaster of the Great Northern. The general offices were now closed, and Ralph had the home of the paymaster in view as his present destination.

A vivid memory of what the torn sheet found in the riddled vest pocket revealed engrossed his mind. That sheet was a scrawl, a letter, or rather what was left of it. Enough of it was there to cause the young railroader to believe that he had made a most important and startling discovery.

The screed was from one scamp in the city to another scamp on the road. Judging from the scrawl, a regular set of scamps had been hired to do some work for high-up, respectable fellows. This work was the securing of certain secret information, the private property of the Great Northern, nothing more--for the present at least.

It seemed, however, that "Jem," in the city, had advised "Rivers," on the road, that now was the great opportunity to work personal graft on the side-- as he designated it. He advised Rivers to keep the regular job going, as five dollars a day was pretty good picking. He, however, added that he must keep close tab on the paymaster deal. It meant a big bag of game. It might not be according to orders, but the other railroad fellows wouldn't lose any sleep if the Great Northern turned up with an empty pay car some fine morning.

The hint was given also that the way to do things right was to get close to the paymaster's system. Such suggestive words as "watching," "papers," appeared in the last lines of the riddled sheet of paper.

"The precious set of rascals," commented Ralph indignantly. "The assistant superintendent knew what he was talking about, it seems. It's all as plain as day to me. Our rivals have employed an irresponsible gang to spy on and cripple our service. Their hirelings are plotting to make a great steal on their own account. Hi, there--mind yourself, will you!"

Ralph was suddenly nearly knocked off his feet. At the moment he was passing along the side of a building used as a restaurant. It was a great lounging place for young loafers, and second class and discharged railroad men.

Its side door had opened forcibly and the big bouncing proprietor of the place was wrathfully chasing a lithe young fellow from the place. His foot barely grazed the latter, who pirouetted on the disturbed Ralph and went sliding across the pavement to the gutter.

"Get out, I tell you, get out!" roared the irate restaurant man. "We don't want the likes of you about here."

"I'm out, ain't I?" pertly demanded the intruder.

"And stay out."

"Yah!"

The man slammed the door, muttered something about stolen tableware and changed eating checks. Ralph did not pause to challenge the ousted intruder further. One glance he had cast at the ugly, leering face of the lad. Then, his lips puckered to an inaudible whistle of surprise and dislike, he hurried his steps.

"Ike Slump!" uttered the young railroader under his breath.

It only needed the presence of the detestable owner of that name to momentarily cause Ralph to feel that the situation was working down to one of absolute peril and intense seriousness. Ike Slump had been a name to conjure by in the past--with the very worst juvenile element in Stanley Junction.

Way back in his first active railroad work, about the first repellant and obnoxious element Ralph had come up against was Ike Slump. When Ralph was given a job in the roundhouse, he had found Ike Slump in the harness. From the very start the latter had made trouble for the new hand.

Ike had tried to direct Ralph wrong, to slight work, to aid him in pulling the wool over the eyes of their superiors in doing poor work. Ralph had manfully refused to be a party to such deception.

A pitched battle had ensued in which Slump was worsted. Later he was discharged, still later he was detected in stealing metal fittings from the roundhouse. After that Ike Slump joined a crowd of regular yard thieves. As Ralph went up the ladder of fortune, Ike went down. He was arrested, escaped, made many attempts to "get even," as he called it, with the boy who had never done him a wrong, and the last Ralph had heard of him he was serving a term in some jail for train wrecking.

How he had got free was a present mystery to Ralph. That he had been pardoned or his sentence remitted through some influence or other was evident, for here was Slump, back in Stanley Junction, where Adair, the road detective, would pick him up in a jiffy, if he was a fugitive from justice.

Ralph had no wish to come in contact with the fellow. On the contrary, so distasteful was Slump and his many ways and his low companions to Ralph, that he was desirous of strictly evading him. Ralph, however, could not help experiencing a new distrust at coming upon Slump at a time when presumptive villainy was in the air.

"Hey!"

Ralph did not pause at the challenge. He realized that Slump had seen and recognized him. He kept straight on, paying no attention to the hail, repeated, but at the corner of two streets, under a lamplight, he halted, for Slump was at his side.

"Well, what do you want?" demanded Ralph bluntly, and with no welcome in his voice.

"I--want to speak to you," stammered Slump, breathless from his run. "I suppose it tickled you nearly to death to see me kicked out of the restaurant back yonder, hey?"

"Why should it?" inquired Ralph.

"That's all right, Fairbanks; natural, too, I suppose, for you never liked me."

"Did you ever give me a chance to try."

"Eh? Well, let that pass. Don't be huffy now. See here."

As Slump spoke, he extended his hands. They were coarse and grimy. With a smirk he inquired:

"See them?"

"See what?" demanded Ralph.

"Clean hands."

"Are they--I didn't understand."

"Yes, sir," declared the young rowdy volubly. "They've worked out the sentence on the stoke pile, and I owe the state nothing. I'm as free in Stanley Junction as any goody-goody boy in the burg, and I want you to know it."

"All right, Ike," said Ralph, pleasantly enough, "hope you'll improve the chance to make good, now you've got the opportunity."

"You bet I will," retorted Slump, with a strangely jubilant chuckle.

"That's good."

"Don't go, I've got something else to say to you."

"I'm pressed for time, Slump--"

"Oh, you can spare me a minute. It may do you some good. Say, you've managed to climb up some while I've been locked up, haven't you?"

"I've had good steady work, yes."

"I'd give an arm for just one run on that dandy Overland Express of yours," observed Slump.

"Why don't you work for it, then," questioned Ralph. "It's in any boy who will attend strictly to business."

"Oh, I don't want the glory," explained Slump.

"What, then?"

"Just one chance to spurt her up till she rattled her old boiler into smithereens and run the whole train into the ditch. That's how much I love the Great Northern!"

Ralph was disgusted. He started down the walk, but Slump was persistent. The latter caught his arm. Ralph allowed himself to be brought to a halt, but determined to break away very shortly.

"Just a word, Fairbanks, before you go," said Slump. "You're going to come across me once in a while, and I want a pleasant understanding, see? You won't see me getting into any more scrapes by holding the bags for others. I'm after the real velvet now, and I'm going to get it, see? I know a heap of what's going on, and something is. I'll give you one tip. I can get you a small fortune to resign your position on the Great Northern."

The way Ike Slump pronounced these words, looking squarely into the eyes of Ralph, could not fail to impress the latter with the conviction that there was some sinister meaning in the proposition. Ralph, however, laughed lightly.

"Thinking of starting a railroad of your own, Slump?" he asked.

"No, I ain't," dissented Slump. "All the same--you see, do you?"

Slump smartly put out one hand curved up like a cup.

"Yes, you told me before," nodded Ralph--"clean hands this time."

"Now, this is a different deal."

"Well?"

"Hollow of my hand--see?"

"I don't."

"Maybe it holds a big railroad system, maybe it don't. Maybe I know a turn or two on the programme where the tap of a finger blows things up, maybe I don't. I only say this: I can fix you right with the right parties--for a consideration. Think it over, see? When you see me again have a little chat with me. It will pay you--see?"

Ralph walked on more slowly after a long wondering stare at Ike Slump. He had never been afraid of the young knave either in a square fight or in a battle of wits. There was something ominous, however, in this new attitude of Slump. He had told just enough to show that something antagonistic to the Great Northern was stirring, and that he was mixed up with it.

The home of the paymaster was located over near the railroad, quite away from the business centre of the town. Ralph reached it after a brisk walk. He found the place dark and apparently untenanted. It looked as if Mr. Little and his family were away, probably at some neighbor's house. Then going around to the side of the house and glancing up at the windows, Ralph discovered something that startled him.

"Hello!" he exclaimed involuntarily, and every sense was on the alert in an instant.

Two flashes inside the downstairs wing of the house, which Ralph knew Mr. Little used as a library, had glinted across the panes of an uncurtained window. Somebody inside the room had scratched a match which went out, then another which stayed lighted.

Its flickerings for a moment illuminated the apartment and revealed two men standing near a desk at one side of the room.

"Why," exclaimed the young railroader--"those mysterious men again!"

CHAPTER VI—IN THE TUNNEL

Ralph pressed close to the window pane of Mr. Little's library room but he did not succeed in seeing much. The last match struck revealed to his sight the two men who had acted so suspiciously the day he had seen them hanging around the Overland Express train with Glen Palmer's grandfather.

If all that he had surmised and discovered was true, it was quite natural that he should come upon them again. Ralph was less startled than surprised. He wondered what their motive could be in visiting the paymaster's house.

"They are not up to burglary," the idea ran through his mind. "It must be they are searching among the paymaster's papers to find out what they can about his system and methods. Yes, that is it."

Ralph saw the man who had struck the matches draw from his pocket a tallow candle, evidently intending to light it. His companion had pulled up the sliding top of a desk and was reaching out toward some pigeon holes to inspect their contents. Just then an unexpected climax came.

The foot of the young railroader slipped on a patch of frozen grass as he pressed too close to the window. Ralph fell up against this with a slight clatter. The man with the match turned very sharply and suddenly. He glared hard at the source of the commotion. He must have caught sight of Ralph's face before the latter had time to draw back, for he uttered a startled ejaculation.

With a bang the desk top fell back in place, the match went out, and the man with the candle fired it wildly at the form at the window with sufficient force to penetrate the pane with a slight crash.

Ralph drew back, some fine splinters of glass striking his face. It was totally dark now in the room into which he had peered. He could catch the heavy tramping of feet in flight and a door slammed somewhere in the house.

"Hey, there--what are you up to," challenged Ralph, sharply, as he stood in a puzzled way debating what was best to do. He turned about, to face a powerfully-built man, cane in hand, storming down upon him from the front of the house.

"It is you, Mr. Little?" inquired Ralph quickly.

"Yes, it's me. Who are you? Oh, young Fairbanks," spoke the paymaster, peering closely at Ralph.

"Yes, sir."

"I thought I heard a pane of glass smash--"

"You did. Hurry to the rear, Mr. Little."

"What for?"

"I'll cover the front."

"Why--"

"Two men are in your house. They were just at your desk when I discovered them."

"Two men in the house!"

"I can't explain now, but it is very important that we prevent their escape."

"Burglars! We were all over to supper at wife's folks--"

"Spies, fits the case better, sir--some rival road spite work, maybe. It's serious, as I shall explain to you later."

"There they are. Hey, stop!"

Two figures had cut across the lawn from the rear of the house.

"They are the same men," declared Ralph, and both he and the paymaster put after them.

The fugitives paid no attention to the repeated demands of the paymaster to halt. They crossed a vacant field and suddenly went clear out of sight.

"They've dropped over the wall guarding the north tracks," said Ralph.

"And we'll follow!" declared Mr. Little dauntlessly.

At this point the north branch of the road ran down a steep grade and was walled in for over a thousand feet. Ralph dropped onto the cindered roadbed. Mr. Little more clumsily followed him.

"Where now?" he puffed, as he scrambled to his feet.

"There they go," said Ralph, pointing towards two forms quite plainly revealed in the night light.

"I see them," spoke the paymaster. "They're caged in."

"Unless they take to the tunnel."

"Then we'll take to it, too," insisted Mr. Little. "I'm bound to get those men."

Ralph admired the pluck and persistency of his companion. The paymaster was a big man and a brave one. He had the reputation of generally putting through any job he started on. The young railroader did not entirely share the hopes of his companion, as he saw the two fugitives reach the mouth of the tunnel, and its gloom and darkness swallowed them up like a cloud.

"The mischief!" roared the paymaster, going headlong, his cane hurtling through space as he stumbled over a tie brace. "I've sprained my ankle, I guess, Fairbanks. Don't stop for me. Run those fellows down. There's bound to be a guard at the other end of the tunnel. Call in his help."

Ralph grabbed up the cane where it had fallen and put sturdily after the fugitives. The tunnel slanted quite steeply at its start. It was about an eighth of a mile in length, and single tracked only. Ralph was not entirely familiar with running details on this branch of the Great Northern, but he felt pretty sure that there were no regular trains for several hours after six o'clock.

The men he was pursuing had quite some start of him, and unless he could overtake them before they reached the other end of the tunnel they were as good as lost for the time being. Ralph's thought was that when he had passed the dip of the tunnel, he would be able to make out the forms of the fugitives against the glare of the numerous lights in the switchyards beyond the other entrance.

The young railroader retained possession of the paymaster's cane as a weapon that might come in handy for attack or defense, as the occasion might arise.

It was as black as night in the tunnel, once he got beyond the entrance, and he had to make a blind run of it. The roadbed was none too smooth, and he had to be careful how he picked his steps. The air was close and smoky, and he paused as he went down the sharp grade with no indication whatever through sight or sound of the proximity of the men he was after.

It had occurred to him more than once that the men in advance, if they should happen to glance back, would be able to catch the outlines of his figure against the tunnel outlet. As they did not wish at all to be overhauled, however, Ralph believed they would plan less to attack him than to strain every effort to get into hiding as speedily as possible.

Headed forward at quite a brisk pace, the young railroader came suddenly up against an obstruction. It was human, he felt that. In fact, as he ran into a yielding object he knew the same to be a barrier composed of joined hands of the two fugitives. They had noted or guessed his sharp pursuit of them, had joined each a hand, and spreading out the others practically barricaded the narrow tunnel roadbed so he could in no manner get past them.

"Got him!" spoke a harsh voice in the darkness. Ralph receded and struck out with the cane. He felt that it landed with tremendous force on some one, for a sharp cry ensued. The next instant one of the fugitives pinioned one wrist and the other his remaining wrist.

Ralph swayed and swung to and fro, struggling actively to break away from his captors.

"What now?" rang out at his ear.

"Run him forward."

"He won't run."

"Then give him his quietus."

Ralph felt that a cowardly blow in the dark was pending. He had retained hold of the cane. He tried to use this as a weapon, but the clasp on either wrist was like that of steel. He could only sway the walking stick aimlessly.

A hard fist blow grazed one ear, bringing the blood. Ralph gave an old training ground twist to his supple body, at the same time deftly throwing out one foot. He had succeeded in tripping up his captor on the left, but though the fellow fell he preserved a tenacious grip on the wrist of the plucky young railroader.

"Keep your clutch!" panted the other man. "I'll have him fixed in a jiffy. Thunder! what's coming?"

"A train!"

"Break loose--we're lost!"

Ralph was released suddenly. The man on the right, however, had delivered the blow he had started to deal. It took Ralph across the temple and for a moment dazed and stunned him. He fell directly between the rails.

The two men had darted ahead. He heard one of them call out to hug the wall closely. Then a sharp grinding roar assailed Ralph's ears and he tried to trace out its cause.

"Something is coming," he murmured. His skilled hearing soon determined that it was no locomotive or train, but he was certain that some rail vehicle of light construction was bearing down upon him.

Ralph was so dazed that he could barely collect wit and strength in an endeavor to crawl out of the roadbed. With a swishing grind the approaching car, or whatever it was, tore down the sharp incline.

His sheer helplessness of the instant appalled and amazed Ralph. It seemed minutes instead of seconds before he rolled, crept, crawled over the outside rail. As he did so, with a whang stinging his nerves like needles of fire, one end of the descending object met his suspended foot full force, bending it up under him like a hinge.

Ralph was driven, lifted against the tunnel wall with harsh force. His head struck the wet slimy masonry, causing his brain to whirl anew.

Something swept by him on seeming wings of fleetness. There was a rush of wind that almost took his breath away. Then there sounded out upon the clammy blackness of the tunnel an appalling, unearthly scream.

CHAPTER VII—DANGER SIGNALS

The danger seemed gone, with the passage of the whirling object on wheels that had so narrowly grazed the young railroader, but mystery and vagueness remained in its trail.

"What was it?" Ralph heard one of his late assailants ask.

"A hand car," was the prompt reply. "She must have struck somebody. Did you hear that yell?"

"Yes--run for it. We don't know what may have happened, and we don't want to be caught here if anybody comes to find out what is up."

Ralph was in no condition to follow the fugitives. For a moment he stood trying to rally his scattered senses. The situation was a puzzling and distrustful one. Abruptly he crouched against the wall of the tunnel.

"The hand car," he breathed--"it is coming back!"

As if to emphasize this discovery, a second time and surely nearing him that alarming cry of fright rang out. Again reversed, the hand car whizzed by him. Then in less than twenty seconds it shot forward in the opposite direction once more. Twice it thus passed him, and on each occasion more slowly, and Ralph was able to reason out what was going on.

The hand car was unguided. Someone was aboard, however, but helpless or unable to operate it. Unmistakable demonstrations of its occupancy were furnished in the repetition of the cries that had at first pierced the air, though less frenzied and vivid now than at the start.

Finally seeking and finding the dead level at the exact centre of the tunnel, the hand car appeared to have come to a stop. Ralph shook himself together and proceeded for some little distance forward. He was guided by the sound of low wailings and sobs. He landed finally against the end of the hand car.

"Hello, there!" he challenged.

"O--oh! who is it?" was blubbered out wildly. "O--oh, mister! I did not do it. Teddy Nolan gave it a shove, and away it went--boo-hoo!"

Ralph read the enigma promptly. Mischievous boys at play beyond the north end of the tunnel had been responsible for the sensational descent of the hand car. He groped about it now and discovered a tiny form clinging to the boxed-up gearing in the centre of the car.

"You stay right still where you are," ordered Ralph, as he located the handles of the car and began pumping for speed.

"Oh, yes, sir, I will."

"It's probably too late to think of heading off or overtaking those fellows," decided Ralph, "but I've got to get this hand car out of harm's way."

It was no easy work, single handed working the car up the slant, but Ralph made it finally. He found a watchman dozing in the little shanty near the entrance to the tunnel. The man was oblivious to the fact of the hand car episode, and of course the same as to the two men who had doubtless long since escaped from the tunnel and were now safe from pursuit. Ralph did not waste any time questioning him. As he was ditching the hand car the ragged urchin who had made a slide for life into the tunnel took to his heels and scampered away.

The young railroader thought next of the paymaster. Ralph made a sharp run of it on foot through the tunnel. He did not find Mr. Little where he had left him, but came across him sitting on a bench at the first flagman's crossing, evidently patiently waiting for his return.

"Well, what luck," challenged Mr. Little.

"None at all," reported Ralph, and recited the events of the past fifteen or twenty minutes.

"That's pretty lively going," commented Mr. Little, looking Ralph over with an approving and interested glance. "I managed to limp this far. I've wrenched my foot. I don't think it amounts to much, but it is quite painful. I'll rest here a bit and see if it doesn't mend."

"Shall I help you to the house, Mr. Little?" suggested Ralph.

"Maybe--a little later. I want to know about this business first--the smashed window and those burglars. Come, sit down here on the bench with me and tell me all about it, Fairbanks."

"They are not burglars," asserted Ralph.

"What are they, then?"

"What I hurriedly hinted to you some time back--spies."

"Spies?"

"Yes."

"What do you mean by that?"

"I had better tell you the whole story, Mr. Little."

"That's it, Fairbanks."

Ralph began with the queer-acting trio who had first attracted his suspicions several days previous. He did not leave out the details of his interview with the assistant superintendent at Rockton.

"Why, Fairbanks," exclaimed the paymaster, arising to his feet in positive excitement, "this is a pretty serious business."

"It strikes me that way, sir."

"If these two men were not incidental burglars, and nothing is missing at the house, they were after information."

"Instead of booty, exactly," responded Ralph, in a tone of conviction.

"And if that is true," continued the paymaster, still more wrought up, "they show a system of operation that means some big design in their mind. Give me the help of your shoulder, Fairbanks. I've got to get to the house and to my telephone right away."

A detour of the walled-in runway was necessary in order that they might reach Mr. Little's home. The paymaster limped painfully. Ralph himself winced under the weight of his hand placed upon his shoulder, but he made no complaint. His right arm was growing stiff and the fingers of that hand he had noticed were covered with blood.

By the time they reached the paymaster's home, his family had returned. Mr. Little led Ralph at once to the library and sank into his armchair at the desk.

"Why," he exclaimed after a glance at Ralph, "you are hurt, too."

"Oh, a mere trifle," declared the young engineer with apparent carelessness.

"No, it's something serious--worth attending to right away," insisted the paymaster, and he called to his wife, introduced Ralph, and Mrs. Little led him out to the kitchen.

In true motherly fashion she seated him on a splint bottomed chair at the sink, got a basin of hot water and some towels, some lint and a bottle of liniment, and proceeded to attend to his needs like an expert surgeon.

Where Ralph's hand had swept the steel rail when his assailant in the tunnel had knocked him off his footing, one arm had doubled up under him, his fingers sweeping a bunch of metal splinters. These had criss-crossed the entire back of his hand. Once mended up, Ralph was most solicitous, however, to work his arm freely, fearing a wrench or injury that might temporarily disable him from road duty.

"I've got the superintendent over the 'phone," said Mr. Little, as Ralph reëntered the library. "He's due at an important lodge meeting, and can't get here until after nine o'clock. See here, Fairbanks," with a glance at the injured hand which Ralph kept to his side in an awkward way, "you'd better get home and put that arm in a sling."

"I think myself I'd better have a look at it," acknowledged Ralph. "It feels pretty sore around the shoulder."

"You have a telephone at your house?" inquired the paymaster.

"Yes, sir."

"I may want to call you up. If I don't, I feel pretty sure the superintendent will, when we have talked over affairs."

Mr. Little insisted on his hired man hitching up the family horse to drive Ralph home. Mrs. Fairbanks at a glance read pain and discomfort in her son's face as he entered the sitting room. Ralph set her fears at rest with a hasty explanation. Then after resting a little he told her all about his adventures of the evening.

"It seems as if a railroader must take a double risk all the time," she said in a somewhat regretful tone.

"It's a part of the business to take things as they come, mother," observed Ralph. "It's a fight nowadays in every line where there is progress. The Great Northern is in the right, and will win, and it is my duty to help in the battle."

When he came to look over his injured arm Ralph found a pretty bad bruise near the shoulder. His mother declared that it would need attention for some days to come.

"By which you mean, I suppose," remarked Ralph with a smile, "that you want to coddle me off duty. Can't be done, mother. I must stay on deck as long as I can pull a lever. Ouch!"

Ralph winced as he happened to give his arm a twist.

"You may change your mind by morning, my son," observed Mrs. Fairbanks, with a slight motherly triumph in her tone.

When Ralph arose the next day he remembered those words. His arm was so stiff he could scarcely bend it at the elbow, and his hand was badly swollen. He had just finished breakfast when there came a ring at the telephone, which Ralph answered.

"That you, Fairbanks?" sounded the voice of the paymaster.

"Yes, Mr. Little."

"How is that arm of yours this morning?"

"Not quite as well as I would like it to be."

"I called you up to tell you that you will probably hear from the general superintendent this forenoon," continued Mr. Little.

"About last night's affair I suppose?"

"In a line with that, yes. He was with me for over three hours last night, and he's pretty well stirred up. Your injured arm will be a good excuse for canceling your run for a few days."

"But I have no idea of canceling my run," declared Ralph. "I'll have that arm in working shape when the Overland pulls out today."

"I'm giving you a hint, that's all," answered the paymaster. "I feel pretty sure the superintendent intends to schedule you for special duty."

CHAPTER VIII—THE OLD SWITCH SHANTY

Ralph came out of the house with a thoughtful look on his face. His arm was in a sling and he quite looked the invalid. His mother followed him to the door.

"You see, I was the wisest," spoke Mrs. Fairbanks.

"Yes, mother, you predicted that I wouldn't feel quite so spry this morning as last night. All the same, if it wasn't for the word just sent me by the general superintendent, you would see me on the regular Overland trip."

"It wouldn't be right," dissented Mrs. Fairbanks. "Suppose your arm gave out at a critical moment of your run?"

"I shouldn't let it," declared Ralph. "It puzzles me, though--the word from headquarters."

"It was rather strange," assented his mother.

"The superintendent simply 'phoned me that I was to remain on the invalid list for a day or two. He said he was going to Rockton, and would be back tomorrow morning, and would expect me then at a conference at ten o'clock. In the meantime all I need to do, he said, was to hang around town, show myself about the yards and the general offices, but to be sure to wear my arm in a sling."

"He has some purpose in view in that last direction, believe me, Ralph," said Mrs. Fairbanks.

"Yes," replied the son thoughtfully, "I'm beginning to guess out a certain system in his methods. I shouldn't wonder if something lively were on the programme. Well, I'll try and put on the enforced vacation as the superintendent suggests. Hello, there's a fine hullaballoo!"

Ralph walked down the steps and to the street to trace the cause of a great outcry beyond the cottage grounds. As he passed through the gate he made out a haggard looking urchin standing on the planking of the crossing crying as if his heart would break.

"Why, it's Ted Rollins, our little neighbor who lives over near the flats," said Ralph, recognizing the ragged and begrimed lad.

The latter was half bent over as if squinting through the cracks in the sidewalk. Then he would let out a yell of distress, dig his fingers into his eyes, resume his looking, and wind up with a kind of frenzied dance, bewailing some direful disaster at the top of his voice. Ralph approached him unobserved.

"Hello, there," he hailed, "what's the trouble here?"

"I've lost it!" wailed the little fellow, without looking up. "It slipped out of my ha-a-and."

"What did?"

"A nickel."

"A nickel?"

"Yes, I earned it, and it rolled down one of those cracks in the sidewalk."

"Which one?" inquired Ralph.

"Don't know which one--boo-hoo! and say--it was for you."

For the first time the weeping lad, glancing up through his tears, recognized Ralph. He instantly dug his hand down into a pocket and began groping there.

"What was for me?" asked Ralph, "the nickel?"

"No, not the nickel, that was for me. The note was for you, though, that I got the nickel to fetch--that I don't get the nickel for fetching, though I fetched it," added Ted Rollins dolefully. "That's it."

The lad brought out a folded creased slip of paper wet with his tears and grimed with contact with his fingers. He extended this to Ralph.

"For me, eh?" he inquired wonderingly.

"Yes, 'Ralph Fairbanks,' he said. He asked me if I knew Ralph Fairbanks, and I said you bet I did. 'Why,' says I, 'he's a regular friend of mine.'"

"That's right, Ted," said Ralph.

"Then he gave me the nickel and the note."

"Who did?"

"The boy."

"What boy?"

"The one I'm telling you about. I never saw him before. He was down near the elevator tracks where the old switch tower shanty is, you know."

"Why, yes, I know," assented Ralph, "but I can't imagine who the note can be from. Oh, I understand now," added Ralph, his eye brightening as he opened the note and caught a glimpse of the signature. "Here, Ted, there's a dime for your faithfulness, and maybe you can find a chum with a big axe who will pry up a few of those sidewalk spikes, and if you find the lost nickel you can have that, too."

"You're a capital fellow, Ralph Fairbanks," cried the delighted little urchin. "If you ever run for president of the Great Northern, my sister says the whole town will vote for you."

"Thank you, Ted," laughed the young railroader, "but they don't elect railroad presidents that way."

"Dad says you'll get there, anyway."

"Thank you again," said Ralph, and as Ted darted away he gave his full attention to the note. It ran:

"Ralph Fairbanks:

"Will you please come to the place where the bearer of this note will direct you, and oblige. I have some money for you.

--Glen Palmer."

"Well, well," said Ralph in a pleased way, "this is pretty quick action on the part of our young chicken raiser. Of course I'll go. Glen Palmer is straight, as I thought he would be. I'm curious to know how he came out with his investment, and doubly curious to learn something about that mysterious old grandfather of his."

Ralph did not need any guide to reach the elevated tracks and the old switch tower shanty alluded to by Ted Rollins. The spot had been a busy one before they straightened out a lot of useless curves and changed the main line a half mile farther south. The old main tracks, however, were still used for switching and standing freights, and there were several grain elevators in the vicinity. It was now a remote and isolated spot so far as general traffic was concerned.

Ralph crossed over a stretch of bleak prairie, leaped a drainage ditch, and started down a siding that was used as a repair track. Just as he reached the end of a freight car he hastened his steps.

Not fifty yards distant two animated figures suddenly filled his range of vision. They were boys. One was Glen Palmer. The other Ralph was amazed to recognize as Ike Slump.

Glen had a broken-off broom in one hand and a bag pretty well filled over his shoulder. He was warding off the approach of Slump, who seemed bent on pestering him from malice or robbing him for profit. Ralph ran forward to the rescue of his young protege, who was no match in strength or size for the bully.

He was not in time to prevent a sharp climax to the scene. Glen swung the heavy bag he carried around to deal his tormenter a blow. Slump either drew a knife or had one concealed up his sleeve all along. At any rate he caught the circling bag on the fly. The knife blade met its bulging surface and slit it woefully, so that a stream of golden grain poured out.

"You ought to be ashamed of yourself!" burst out Glen Palmer, indignantly.

"Strangers pay toll around here, or I know the reason," derided bad Ike Slump.

"Just drop that, Slump," spoke Ralph, stepping forward.

"Humph!" growled Ike, retreating a step or two and looking rather embarrassed. "I didn't expect you."

"I see you didn't," observed Ralph. "This petty business doesn't seem to accord very well with your high pretentions of last evening."

"He has wasted all my grain!" cried Glen, tears starting to his eyes. "He said I'd have to pay toll to the gang, whatever that is, if I came around here gathering up chicken feed, and the flagman yonder has given me permission to sweep out all the cars after they have emptied at the elevators."

"Don't worry," said Ralph, reassuringly. "I will see to it that you are not interfered with, that your rights are respected after this."

"Huh!" scoffed Ike, and then with a great start and in a sharp change of voice he shouted out, "Hello, I say, hello!"

Ike stood staring fixedly at Glen at the moment. The latter in rearranging his disordered attire for the first time had removed the broad peaked cap he wore. The instant he caught Ike's piercing glance fixed upon him, Glen flushed and in great haste replaced the cap, quite screening his face and turned away.

"Aha!" resumed Ike, continuing to stare at Glen. "Why, when, where--drat me!" and he struck his head with his hand, as if trying to drive out some puzzling idea. "Say, I've seen you before. Where? I never forget faces. Wallop me! but I know you, and--"

Just then Slump was walloped. The flagman at the shanty one hundred feet away had evidently witnessed the tussle between the two boys. That he was a friend to Glen was indisputable, for coming upon the scene from between two lines of freight he pounced on Slump, whacking him smartly about his legs with his flag stick.

"You pestering loafer, out of here," he shouted, "or I'll break every bone in your body," and Slump ran down the track precipitately.

He paused only once, at a safe distance from pursuit. It was to shake his fist at the watchman, then to wave it in a kind of threatening triumph at Ralph, and then to make a speaking trumpet of his hand and to yell through it.

"I know that boy, don't you forget it, and I'll see you later."

Ralph wondered a good deal at this demonstration. Then he turned to Glen.

"Why," he exclaimed, noticing that the face of the latter was as white as chalk and that he was trembling all over. "What's the matter, Glen?"

"I--that--is that fellow upset me," stammered Glen, failing to meet Ralph's scrutinizing glance.

"Something more than that, Glen," insisted Ralph. "You act half scared to death. Do you know Ike Slump?"

"No."

"Did you ever meet him before?"

"Never," declared Glen strenuously.

Ralph had to be satisfied with this. Glen turned from him as if to hide some emotion or embarrassment. He began tying up his bag so as to cover the slit made in it by Slump's knife and scooped up the scattered grain.

"Wait till I get this gathered up and I want to talk with you," he said.

A new figure came lounging leisurely down the track as the watchman proceeded to his shanty. Ralph recognized Dan Lacey, a ne'er-do-well who had tried about every department of railroad service inside of two years and had failed signally in every attempt.

He was a good-natured, indolent fellow, perfectly harmless and generally popular. He halted in front of Ralph with a speculative glance at Glen Palmer.

"Howdy, Fairbanks," he hailed. "Say, pet of yours yonder, I understand."

"Who--Glen Palmer?"

"Yes, that's his name."

"He seems to be a fine young fellow I helped out a little."

"Always doing that. Know him pretty well?"

"Hardly at all."

"Well," drawled Lacey taking in Glen with a continuous analyzing glance, "he's a cracker jack."

"What do you mean, Lacey?"

"Telegraphy. I've seen some pretty swell operators in my time, but that kid--say, believe me, Fairbanks, he's got the last one of them backed clear off the board."

CHAPTER IX—A SUSPICIOUS DISCOVERY

"Explain yourself, Lacey," directed the young railroader.

"Nothing to explain--it's exactly as I say. That lad's a wonder."

"At telegraphing, you said."

"At telegraphing, I mean."

"How do you know?"

"Heard him, saw him."

"When, where?"

"Just a little bit ago up at the old switch tower. You know they left one or two broken instruments there when they moved the general outfit. Wires down, but one or two good sharp keys still in place. I was snoozing on the bench outside. Suddenly--click! click! Then the regular call. Then the emergency--say, I thought I was back at Dover with old Joslyn Drake, the crack operator of the Midland Central. You know I put in a year at the key. Not much at it myself, but you bet your life I can tell fine work. Why, that lad ran the roll like a veteran. Then he began on speed. I crept closer. There he was, thinking no one saw him, rattling the key till it pounded like a piston on a sixty mile an hour run."

Ralph was a good deal astonished. Glen was a pretty young fellow to line up in the way that Dan Lacey described. Then a kind of vague disagreeable idea came into the mind of the young railroader. He recalled the old grandfather and his two villainous associates, for such they had proved themselves to be the evening previous.

"Things are dovetailing in a queer sort of way," reflected Ralph. "Perhaps a little investigation will give me a clew as to those fellows who slipped me in the tunnel."

When he had gathered up the scattered grain Glen Palmer glanced uneasily all about him as if looking for Ike Slump. Then he became his natural self.

"I'm awfully glad to see you," he said to Ralph, "although it seems as if there's a fight or a smashup, or some outlandish thing on the books every time I meet you."

"Well that doesn't matter so long as you come out of it all right, eh, Glen?" propounded Ralph brightly.

"You're a good champion in the nick of time," declared Glen. "I wanted to see you, so I took the liberty of sending for you."

"Why didn't you come up to the house?"

"Oh, no! no!----" began Glen with a start. "That is--I don't go to town much. I've got some money for you. There are ten dollars. I'll have the balance Saturday."

Ralph accepted the bank bills which Glen extended.

"I'll hand this to Mr. Fry," he said. "You don't need to pay it now, though, Glen."

"Oh, yes, I want to get out of debt as fast as I can."

"You're starting out the right way to do it. Pretty quick action you got on your chicken deal, it seems to me."

"Oh, that was luck," explained Glen, brightening up. "There was one special lot among the chickens, about twenty-four of them. They were in a tier of the car that wasn't battered in the smash up. We got them all out safe and sound. They are of a rare breed--they call them Blue Cochins."

"Valuable?"

"I didn't know till after we got them down to the farm. A man driving by noticed them. They have black eyes instead of the usual red ones, and he said they were very scarce. The next day he came down and offered me five dollars each for two settings of their eggs. Think of it--nearly a half a dollar an egg. I delivered them yesterday, and the man said there are any number of people who would buy the eggs if they knew I had them, and about the choice breed."

"Why, this is interesting," said Ralph.

"Say, can't you come down and see my layout?" inquired Glen eagerly. "I'd be dreadfully glad."

"Why, I might," replied Ralph thoughtfully, consulting his watch.

"There's our chance, if you will," said Glen, grabbing the arm of his companion and indicating a short freight train just pulling off from a side switch. "It's three miles and a half to the farm, and that train goes within a short distance of it."

They ran for the train. It was composed of empties with a caboose attached. Aboard of this the boys clambered and sat down on the rear platform.

"I come down here for the sweepings every morning," said Glen. "To-day and one other day in the week there isn't much to get. One day I got over two bushels and a half, though."

"That's pretty fine," commented Ralph.

"It's a big item in my feed bill, I can tell you," declared Glen. "I've got a new arrangement in view, too--the grain inspector at Stanley Junction."

"Yes, I know him," nodded Ralph.

"Well, my good friend the flagman here introduced him day before yesterday, and he told me that all those little bags containing samples are thrown into a big bin and dumped into the dust heap when they're past inspection. After this he's going to have them left in the bin, and I'm going to arrange to have a cartman call once a week and haul the stuff out to the farm."

"Friends everywhere, eh, Glen," said Ralph encouragingly.

"I'm so glad!" murmured his companion in a low grateful tone.

The young railroader calculated that he could visit the farm and get back to Stanley Junction by noon time. At the end of a three miles' jerky run the train slowed down at a crossing and Ralph and Glen left it.

"There's the place," said the latter, as they reached the end of a grove, and he pointed to an old, low-built ruin of a house just ahead of them.

"They call it Desolation Patch around here. It's in litigation somehow, and no one has lived in it until we came for several years, they tell me."

"It does look rather ragged, for a fact," said Ralph. "How did you come to pick it out, Glen?"

"Oh, it was just the place I was looking for. You see," explained the boy in a slightly embarrassed way, "my grandfather is sort of--queer," and Glen pointed soberly to his head.

"Yes, I understand," nodded Ralph.

"I didn't want to take him to a town where he might be noticed and mightn't feel at home. Then there were reasons which--yes, some reasons."

Ralph did not ask what they were. The farm embraced some twenty acres. Its improvements were mostly rickety, broken down barns and sheds. These seemed to be utilized in the chicken industry to the last foot of available space, the interested visitor noticed. An enclosure formed of sections of old wire netting held over a hundred of the feathery brood, and some of the boxes obtained from the wreck had been made into brooding pens.

Then Ralph laughed outright as he noticed two, four, half a dozen chickens limping about cheerfully with a stick taking the place of one broken or missing foot, and at others with a wing in splints.

"What do you think of it?" inquired Glen eagerly.

"I think you're a rare genius," declared Ralph, slapping his companion heartily on the shoulder.

"There are some neighbors beyond here who have been awfully kind to us," proceeded Glen. "They gave us an old cooking stove and other kitchen things, and now that we have the chickens and eggs we can trade in the neighborhood for most everything we want. We have plenty to eat--oh, you did a big thing the day you went bail for me on this chicken deal."

Glen went into details about his business when they reached the house. He showed Ralph a book in which he had enumerated his various belongings. Then he made an estimate of what sixty days' chicken farming would result in. The exhibit made Ralph dizzy. It was fowls and eggs and multiples of fowls and eggs in exact but bewildering profusion.

"You're heading right, that's sure," applauded Ralph. "What's that room for?"

Ralph was glancing into an adjoining apartment with a great deal of curiosity and interest. He had never seen such a room before. It held two rudely-constructed tables, and attached to these were some old telegraph instruments, just like the abandoned ones down at the old division tower shanty. Pieces of wire ran to the ceiling of the room, but no farther. On the wall above one of the tables was a great sheet of paper covered with a skeleton outline system.

Somewhere Ralph had seen a picture of a rude frontier train dispatcher's office. This was almost a perfect counterpart of it. He fixed his eyes in questioning wonderment on his companion. Glen looked somewhat embarrassed and flushed up. Then with an affected laugh he said:

"This is my grandfather's den."

"But--the telegraph instruments, the wires?"

"Why, grandfather was once a telegrapher, a famous----" He checked himself. "This is his hobby, and I fixed up things to please him."

"How about yourself?" asked Ralph, with a keen glance at his companion, recalling what Dan Lacey had told him back at the switch shanty.

Glen eyed him steadily for a moment. Then his eyes faltered.

"My grandfather has taught me a lot about telegraphy," he admitted.

Ralph walked over to the chart on the wall. The young engineer had learned his Morse alphabet early in his railroad career, and knew something of the system in vogue along the line.

As his eye studied the rude scrawl made with a red pencil, Ralph at once discerned that its dotted lines denoted three divisions of a railway system. From separate dots he traced a line of towns. Above each was a designation, an initial, a double initial, sometimes an additional numeral.

"The mischief!" muttered the young railroad engineer under his breath, "this doesn't look much like a plaything outfit. Why, that is a perfect transcript of the routing chart in the train dispatcher's office at Stanley Junction."

CHAPTER X—THE TRAIN DISPATCHER

A great flood of dark suspicion crossed Ralph's mind at the discovery of the road chart. A dozen quick questions arose to his lips. Before he could speak, however, there was a hail from the outside.

"Hey, there, young fellow!"

Glen ran out to the road where a farm hand on horseback had halted. Ralph followed him.

"About your old man," spoke the visitor.

"My grandfather, yes," said Glen breathlessly.

"You told us to sort of keep an eye on him. He came down to our place about an hour ago to get some butter. Scruggins, who lives just beyond here was going to Centerville. Your old man said he wanted to go there, too, to see the new swinging signal bridge over the railroad."

"Oh, but you stopped him."

"I was away when it happened, and he would not listen to ma. Scruggins said he would bring him back all right."

"Oh, I must stop him! I must overtake him!" cried Glen in such poignant distress that Ralph was surprised. "Grandfather was away nearly two days before, and pretty near got lost, and I was worried to death. I must go after him, indeed I must! Excuse me, won't you," he pleaded of Ralph.

"I will see you again soon," answered Ralph.

"Do--sure," said Glen. "I have lots to tell you."

The farm hand rode on his way and Glen ran down the road on foot at great speed. Ralph went back slowly to the open house. Once more he inspected the telegraph room. Then with a good deal of thoughtfulness he started homeward.

"There's something queer about all this business," ruminated the young railroader. "That boy's grandfather was certainly in with the two men who escaped from me in the tunnel. He is an expert telegrapher. So is Glen. Ike Slump had something up his sleeve about Glen. That chart of the road has the regular telegraph signal on it. What does this all mean?"

Ralph could not believe that Glen was a schemer or anything of that sort. For all that, there was a decided mystery about him. He seemed to be afraid of Slump, appeared to shun the town and its people. Why was he wandering all about the country with a helpless old man? Why had he flushed up and acted embarrassed when Ralph had asked him several pointed questions?

"Glen must certainly be questioned about the two men who had his grandfather in tow," decided Ralph, "for those fellows must be located and watched. I wish Bob Adair was here. He would soon let light in on the whole affair. I'd rather he would do it, for I feel very friendly towards Glen and I don't like hurting his feelings by seeming to pry into his private business."

Ralph rested a few minutes on the porch when he reached home and then started down town. He was in a certain state of suspense, for the orders of the general superintendent were vague and unsatisfactory. Something was working, Ralph felt, in which he was to take an active part. The paymaster had indicated that affairs were being stirred up. Idleness and suspense worried the young railroader, however, and he anxiously awaited the coming interview with his superior officer.

Ralph went down to the roundhouse and met many of his friends. Old Forgan, the fireman, described the disgust and dejection of Fogg at having a new running mate. Everybody had heard that Ralph had a layoff on account of a fall disabling him, and his arm in the sling won him a good deal of friendly sympathy. He made a tour of the general offices to learn that Mr. Little was laid up at home with a lame foot, and that the general superintendent was out of town.

Ralph had the free run of the general offices, as the saying went. He was ambitious, energetic and popular, and the busiest man in the service had a pleasant nod and a kindly word for him as he went around the different departments. When he arrived at the train dispatcher's office, the young railroader went in and sat down.

Ralph was in one of the most inviting places a man can get into, especially if he is interested in the workings of a big railway system.

The thought came to him, as he sat watching the men who held in their keeping the lives of thousands of passengers, that not all the credit for a good swift run was due to the engineer and train crew. He smiled as he recalled how the newspapers told every day of the President or some big functionary out on a trip, and how at the end of the run he stopped beside the panting engine, and reaching up to shake the hand of the faithful, grimy engineer, would say:

"Thank you so much for giving us a good run. I don't know when I have ridden so fast before," or words to that effect.

The reader of such items never thinks the engineer and crew are mere mechanical agents, small cogs in a huge machine. They do their part well, but the little office of the train dispatcher is a red-hot place where they have a red-hot time, where one tap of the sounder may cover the fate of numberless extras, specials and delayed trains.

The young engineer took particular notice of the dispatcher's office on the present occasion. This was because so much of pending trouble seemed to involve the wire system of the Great Northern. The wire tapping episode, the prototype routing chart at the chicken farm, had aroused suspicion in his mind. Then, too, Ralph had often had a fondness and an admiration for this branch of the service. At one time, in fact, he had studied telegraphy with the purpose in view of following it up, and old John Glidden, a fast friend of his, had invited him to the dispatcher's office and had taught him a great many useful things in his line.

Glidden was the first trick dispatcher and was not on duty just now. Ralph nodded to two subordinates at their tables, and snuggled back into his comfortable seat with the time and interest to look over things.

The interior of the dispatcher's office was not very sumptuous. There was a big counter at one side of the room. This contained the train register, car record books, message blanks and forms for various reports. Against the wall on one of the other sides was a big blackboard known as the call board. Ralph read here the record of the probable arrival and departure of trains and the names of their crews. Also the time certain crews were to be called.

About the middle of the room in the recess of a bay window was the dispatcher's table. Ralph only casually knew the man in charge. His name was Thorpe, a newcomer, and an expert in his line, but gruff and uncivil in the extreme, and he had few friends. In front of him was the train sheet containing information exact and absolute in its nature of each train on the division. On the sheet was also a space set apart for the expected arrival of trains from the other end and one for delays. Glidden had once gone over one of these sheets with Ralph with its loads, empties and miscellaneous details, and Ralph knew that the grim, silent man at the table must know the precise location of every train at a given moment, how her engine was working, how she had done along the road, and all about her engineer and conductor.

Ralph spent nearly a half an hour in the dispatcher's room. Then he went down to the depot. An extra was just leaving for the west. He paused to have a cheery word with the engineer and fireman, whom he knew quite well. They were getting ready for the orders to pull out, when the three of them stared hard at a flying form coming down the track.

"Hello," observed the engineer, "it's Bates."

"Yes, the second trick man in the dispatcher's office," nodded the fireman. "Wonder what's up with him?"

"Something is," declared Ralph, "according to his looks and actions."

Bates came puffing up white and breathless. Evidently he had just got out of bed, half dressed himself, put on a pair of slippers, no coat, no hat, and he seemed to ignore the cold and snow amid some frantic urgency of reaching the departing train.

"Say!" he panted, approaching the fireman who was giving No. 341 the last touch of oil before they pulled out, "thank heaven you haven't gone!"

"Hey?" stared the engineer.

"Don't pull out for a minute."

"Why not?"

"I think there's a mistake in your orders."

"What's the matter with you?" snapped back the fireman with affected gruffness. "I hain't got no orders. Come here, till I oil the wheels in your head."

"You must come up to the dispatcher's office," insisted Bates urgently, and the engineer followed him wonderingly. Ralph, tracing something unusual in the episode of the moment, kept them company.

The chief dispatcher was standing by the counter. He glanced sharply at Bates with the words:

"What's up, kid? Seen a ghost? You look almost pale enough yourself to be one."

"No," quavered Bates in a shaky tone. "I haven't seen any ghosts, but I am afraid I forgot to notify that track gang just west of here about this extra."

The chief went to the order book and glanced at the train sheet.

"Oh, bosh!" he said. "Of course you notified them. Here it is as big as life. Look out for extra west engine 341 leaving Stanley Junction at 1:21 P. M. What do you want to get a case of rattles and scare us all that way for. Say, I'd ought to run down your spinal column with a rake. Don't you know there are other dispatchers in this office besides yourself--men who know more in a minute about the business than you do in a month? Don't you suppose that order book would be verified and the train sheet consulted before sending out the extra. Say, don't you ever show up with such a case of rattles again."

Bates expressed an enormous sigh of relief. As he came down to the platform, however, Ralph noticed that he was shaking from head to foot.

"Did you ever work up there?" inquired Bates in a solemn tone.

"No," answered Ralph.

"Then don't. Just wake up once after you've left the key, and get thinking you've forgotten something, and--nightmare? Fairbanks, it's worse than the horrors!"

CHAPTER XI—MAKING A SCHEDULE

"You understand me, Fairbanks?"

"Perfectly, Mr. Drake."

"You have helped us out of trouble before this and I believe you can be of inestimable service in the present instance. We are sorry to lose a first-class engineer, but we need you somewhere else, and need you badly."

They were seated in the private office of the superintendent of the Great Northern, that august official and the young engineer of the Overland Express, and a long, earnest and serious colloquy had just ended.

"From what I have told you and from what you have personally discovered, it is more than apparent that a plot is on foot among our train dispatchers to cripple the running time of the road for the benefit of the opposition."

"There is little doubt of that, I think," said Ralph.

"There is a leak somewhere, and it must be stopped."

"It is my opinion that investigations should begin at the fountain head," submitted Ralph.

"That is just where we shall begin. It may be a hard, even a dangerous task. We look to you, Fairbanks, for results."

It was the third day after Ralph's adventure in the tunnel. Not much had happened of active importance during that time. Ralph had met the superintendent on three different occasions. The present one was a definite culmination of a series.

The young railroader felt very much pleased at the confidence placed in him by the railroad head. It stirred his pride because it had all come about naturally. The superintendent had told him that after a little preliminary work he was to be made chief dispatcher of the Western division of the road. It was a grand promotion, both in importance and salary, enough to satisfy the most ambitious person working for a rapid rise.

Ralph had been sent to the home of the paymaster by the superintendent, and there was a colloquy there. Bob Adair, the road detective, was called in from the other end of the line, and Ralph told him the story of Glen Palmer and his grandfather, leaving the officer to work out himself whatever mystery might surround the two.

In plain words, somebody was tampering with the train dispatching service of the road. Some one on the inside was giving out important information. Cross orders had gone over the wires in a mysterious way and could not be traced. There had been two bad freight wrecks, and twice the Overland

Express had been caught in a tangle brought about by vague contradictory orders and had come in many hours late.

As to those who were suspected of being responsible for this state of affairs Ralph was apprized in his talks with the superintendent. The plans to trap them and fasten the proofs of conspiracy upon them were all outlined to the young railroader. Ralph had blocked out just what he was expected to do, but that day as he was led to the office of the train dispatcher by the superintendent he knew that he had no easy task before him.

Glidden was in charge as they came into the place. The two trick men under him and the copy operators were busy at their tables. Mounted on a roll in front of Glidden was the current official time card of the division. From the information contained thereon he had evidently just finished his calculation for time orders, meeting points and work trains.

"Good morning, Glidden," said the superintendent. "I spoke to you yesterday about our friend, Fairbanks here."

The gruff dispatcher nodded brusquely. He liked Ralph and the latter knew it. Ralph also knew that Glidden was one of the "true blues" of the office.

"His arm is not strong enough to pull a lever, but he's in shape to tackle a key, and knows how to do it."

"Glad," vouchsafed Glidden tersely.

"All right. Set him at work."

"Come on," said Glidden, and he opened the little office gate and Ralph stood within the charmed precincts of the train dispatching circle.

"You've had some experience, I understand," resumed Glidden, after some bustling about. "I suppose you know what an O. S. report is?"

"The one sent in by operators of the various stations as trains arrive and depart."

"Exactly, and the 'Consists'?"

"The conductors' messages giving the exact composition and destination of every car in the train."

"You'll do," nodded Glidden. "Now, then, I have an inkling you and I are booked for something special at the relay station to-night, so you needn't work yourself out. Just for practice, though, and to prove how smart you are, show the kind of stuff you are made of by tackling that."

Glidden threw down a train sheet before Ralph, and following it a copied telegram. Then he strode away, with the words:

"Make out a schedule for this special, giving her a clean sweep from end to end with the exception of No. 8."

"Very well, Mr. Glidden," said Ralph quietly. "How soon do you want it?"

"Take your time," was the short reply, while a chuckle sounded deep down in the throat of the dispatcher.

Ralph set his lips grimly. He realized that for a green hand he had been given an arduous task. He knew much about the service, however, and had not watched, studied and absorbed during the past two days for nothing. He was fully determined that this special should have "a run for her money." If she ran on his schedule, no train load was going away with the idea that the Great Northern was not the swiftest road of the bunch if he could help it, and Ralph had a big idea that he could.

Glidden sent over a copy operator, a young fellow who agreed to do the copying while Ralph made the schedule. There was a whimsical twinkle in his eye, but Ralph dauntlessly started in at his work.

The special in question was to be whooped through that afternoon, the run was one hundred and two miles, with plenty of sidings and passing tracks, and besides, old Dan Lacey, with engine No. 86, was on, so he could be sure of a run that was a hummer.

The superintendent came into the office for a moment to see what Ralph was at, and said carelessly:

"Tear things loose, Fairbanks. There's a Congressional Railroad Committee aboard of that special. Make 'em all car sick."

Ralph took the train sheet and familiarized himself with its every detail. Down its centre was printed the names of all the stations on the division and the distances between them. On either side of the main column were ruled smaller columns, each one of which represented a train. The number of each train was at the head of the appropriate column, and under it the names of the conductor and engineer and the number of loads and empties on the train.

All trains on the division were arranged in three classes, and as Ralph knew had certain rights. Trains of the first class were passengers. The through freight and combination freight and passenger made up the second class. All other trains, such as local freights, work trains and construction trains, composed the third class.

Ralph began his calculating on the basis of the invariable rule in force on all railroads, that trains running one way have the exclusive right over trains of their own and inferior classes running in the opposite direction. Ralph began his work by framing up the initial order:

"Order number 29

To G. N. E.--all trains

G. N. R. R. (Western Division)

Dispatcher's office

D. S.

Special east engine No. 86 will run from Rockton to Dover, having right of track over all trains except No. 8 on the following schedule:

Leave Rockton 3:12 P. M.

There Ralph paused.

"Stuck," insinuated his copy operator with a grin.

"No, only thinking," declared Ralph.

Here was where the figuring came in, along with the knowledge of the road, grades and the like, in which Ralph was by no means lacking, for he knew familiarly nearly every foot of the way out of Rockton. He studied and used up lots of gray matter and even chewed up a pencil or two. Ralph read his schedule carefully and handed it to the second trick operator. The latter knitted his brows for a moment and then slowly said:

"For a beginner that's the best schedule I ever saw."

"Thank you," bowed Ralph modestly.

"It's a hummer, without a doubt. To prevent the lives of the Congressional Committee being placed in peril, though, I think you had better make another."

"Think so?" questioned Ralph blankly.

"You see," went on the operator solemnly, "you have only allowed seven minutes between Lisle and Hull, while the time card shows the distance to be six miles. Dan Lacey and his engine 86 are capable of great bursts of speed, but they can't fly. Then there's the through. She's an hour late from the south today. What are you going to do about her. Pass them on one track, I suppose?"

"He's guying you, Fairbanks," spoke a gruff but pleased voice at Ralph's shoulder. "Lacey can make the spurt without a quiver, and as you probably noticed the late through is cancelled for transfer at Blakeville. You'll do."

Ralph picked up a good deal of general information that day. He perfected himself in the double-order system. This covered the giving of an order to all trains concerned at the same time. A case came up where the dispatcher desired to make a meeting point for two trains. The order was sent simultaneously to both of them. Ralph had a case in point where a train was leaving his end of the division and wherein it was necessary to make a meeting point with a train coming in. Before giving his order to his conductor and engineer he telegraphed to a station at which the incoming train would soon arrive. From there the operator repeated the message back word for word, giving a signal that his red board was turned. By this means both trains received the same order and there would be no doubt about the point at which they were to meet.

Time orders, slow orders, extra orders, annulment orders, clearance orders-- Ralph found that any one gifted with a reasonable amount of common sense and having practical knowledge of the rudiments of mathematics could do the work successfully. Beneath all the simplicity of the system, however, the young railroader realized that there ran a deep undercurrent of complications that only long time and a cool head could master.

All of a sudden sometimes some train out on the road that had been running all right would bob up with a hot box or a broken draw head, and then all the calculations for a new train would be knocked awry.

About four o'clock in the afternoon the superintendent came into the office and made a gesture towards Ralph which the latter understood perfectly. He nudged Glidden as he passed him, who blinked up at him intelligently. Then Ralph went home.

It was just after dusk that the young dispatcher left the cottage. It had set in a cold tempestuous night with blinding snow eddies, and Ralph wore a protecting storm coat, and carried a good lunch in one of its capacious pockets.

He walked about a mile across town until he came to the limits crossing, and stood in the shelter of a flagman's shanty for a few minutes. Then a sharp whistle greeted his ears. He strained his vision and made out a dim form loitering near a big heap of ties.

"Mr. Glidden?" spoke Ralph, advancing to meet this man.

"That's what," responded Glidden, in his usually snappy way. "All ready?"

"Yes."

"It's all arranged. The regular men have been called off for the night. You take the relay station, and I'll be on duty at the tower station beyond, catching the messages that fly over the wires, and see if we can't nail the people who are making the Great Northern all this trouble."

CHAPTER XII—AT THE RELAY STATION

The relay station was located just beyond the limits of Stanley Junction, and was practically the feeder through which ran all the railroad and commercial wires focussing at headquarters. It stood in a wide triangle formed by the tracks of the three divisions of the road, which here branched out north, south and west.

The station was the top of a sort of wareroom for all kinds of railroad junk. Stairs led up to it both inside and outside. Over the tower roof, reached by a trap door, was the great enclosed network of wires covering all the lines of the Great Northern.

Ralph had talked affairs over so closely with the superintendent and later with Glidden, that as he left the latter he knew just what he was expected to do and how he was to do it. His mission was one of great importance and of secrecy as well, for the relay station and the first switch tower on the southern branch less than a quarter of a mile beyond it, were suspected points in the train dispatching service just now.

Ralph left Glidden after a brief whispered conversation. He gained the immediate vicinity of the relay station through slow, cautious progress. He had visited the place the day previous and had studied his ground well. When he at length entered the open doorway, he felt sure that he had reached his goal without attracting the attention of the two occupants of the operating room whom he had made out as he approached.

Ralph did not go up the stairs outside or inside. About twelve feet aloft and gained by a ladder of cleats nailed across two supports was a platform. It abutted the operating room, and it seemed to be a catch-all for half reels of wire, insulators and other material used in the telegraphic line. Ralph reached this, and taking great care not to disturb anything that might make a racket, he crept directly up to a window looking into the operating room.

This window was used for ventilation in summer. Just now it was crusted with dust and cob-webbed so that while he could look beyond its grimy panes, there was little danger of his being seen from within. Better than that, he noted that a broken upper pane had one corner gone, and he could distinctly hear every sound made in the operating room.

There were two men in the place. One of them was the night operator. Against this fellow Ralph had been warned. He had a face that would naturally excite suspicion, and he was familiarly known as Grizzly. He was seated at the operating table ready for duty.

The man beside him had no business there, so far as Ralph could figure out. He looked like a rough workman, but his easy bearing showed that he was on an equality with the operator. His companion addressed him as Mason.

This fellow, lounging lazily near the little stove that heated the place and smoking a short stump of a pipe, opened the conversation with the words:

"Cozy for the night, Grizzly."

"Looks it. The split trick man gave his D. S. good night, and is gone."

"Who is he?"

"New man."

"Isn't that suspicious--so many new men lately?"

"Oh, I'm posted and watching out for squalls. Think he's a new one from another road. Works like a ham factory hand. When he turned out his first message I asked which foot he did it with. The way he looked at the time cards where the calls are printed and kept the key open, I knew he was an innocent greenhorn. Didn't know what 30 meant when it came, got rattled when headquarters was on the quad, and stumbled over the pink almost scared to death."

A week previous all this would have been Greek to Ralph. At present he quickly understood that 30 was the end of a long message, the quad was where they sent four messages at a time, and a pink was a rush telegram.

"Then you think you're not being watched?" inquired Mason.

"Sure of it," responded Grizzly with confidence.

"What's the cross orders from our friends?"

"Nothing on the general mix up plan," reported the operator. "They struck the right man when they hit me to help them. I've got a big hunch for the far west, and wouldn't have cared if the Great Northern had let me out, since, with the chance to carry a big wad of money away with me, why of course I'm in trim for whatever blows along."

"What's special to-night?"

"A side trick, and that's why I sent for you. We made a bad mix up two nights ago with cross orders and tappings. I think it aroused the suspicions of the superintendent, so we're going slow on that tack for a few days. The gang working for the rival road, though, have let me in on some of their side games. One of them is due to-night."

"What is it?"

"You'll know when the time comes. Got your tools with you?"

Mason lazily touched a bag at his feet with his toe, and it jangled as he replied.

"All of them."

"Good, enjoy yourself till about eleven o'clock. If anyone comes duck behind the box yonder, though I don't think there's any chance of a visit a night like this. The bosses are paying too much attention to the stock end of traffic deals to take a flight at a little disruption of the service. There's a nine-- Train orders, I've got to go at my routine."

Ralph settled down as comfortably as he could in his secure hiding place. What he had just heard confirmed forever suspicions that crooked work was being done by crooked operators, and that this fellow Grizzly was one of them.

He listened to the monotonous grind out of the operator: "O.S. O.S. X.N. No. 21 a. 7:39, d. 7:41," and knew that the Limited Mail had reached Tipton, and had gone on. The night schedule for the Mountain Division west ran the wires, then miscellaneous messages. All this was like reading a book to Ralph, while his mind formed a mental map, a picture of conditions all along the line.

It grew dreadfully monotonous by nine o'clock, however. Grizzly grumbled while getting a heap of work out of the way, Mason went to sleep and snored in his chair by the stove. A sudden diversion, however, aroused him. There was the sound of the lower outside door slamming shut. Ralph could look down at the stairway. Someone had appeared ascending it. Grizzly heard the footsteps, warning him of an intruder, and rushed at Mason shaking him vigorously with the sharp mandate:

"Bolt!"

A minute later, peering within the operating room, Ralph saw the intruder enter. Mason had got to cover and Grizzly back to his instrument. The intruder suggested some half tipsy ranchman, who staggered into the room shaking the snow from his garments.

"Hi, there, young man," he hailed familiarly to Grizzly. "I want to send a message to Wayne."

"Sorry, but it's too late."

"Too late for what?" growled the intruder, looking skeptical and ugly.

"All the instruments cut out that way and we won't have Wayne till six o'clock in the morning."

"Won't, eh? Well, you've got to, that's all," observed the man, coming nearer to the operating table.

"Come around in the morning and some of the day force will send the message for you."

"No. I've got twenty-six cars of cattle out here that are going there tomorrow, and I want to notify my agents."

Grizzly shook his head and turned to his table. The stranger bolted up against him with a savage face.

"Say," he said, "you send this message or there is going to be trouble."

"Not much, I won't send your confounded old message; get out of this office."

There was a swift movement on the part of the ranchman, then an ominous click, and Grizzly was looking down the barrel of a revolver.

"Give me your blamed old message and I'll send it for you," growled the scared operator, though there was not a wire anywhere near Wayne at the time, but Grizzly had a scheme to stave the fellow off. He took the paper from the man, went over to the switchboard, fumbled at a local instrument, and, as Ralph discerned, went through the form of sending a message.

The stranger watched him furtively, pistol in hand, swaying to and fro like a reed in the wind and grinning like a monkey.

"There, I hope you're satisfied now," muttered Grizzly.

"Of course I am," chuckled the ranchman; "only I rushed a dodge on you, for the pistol isn't loaded. You bit like a fish."

It was the turn of Grizzly to chuckle, however. As the fellow disappeared Mason came into sight again, and the twain chuckled over the deluded ranchman whose message would not go over the wires for many hours to come.

Towards ten o'clock things quieted down. Few messages went over the wires. It was only occasionally that the clicking told off some important train report from big centers. Grizzly looked and acted uneasy. He arose and strode about the room, looking out at the stormy night, stopping dead short in reflective halts, and glancing frequently at the clock, as though he was expecting somebody or something.

"You act as if you was watching for something to happen," suggested Mason, after a long spell of silence.

"I am," replied the operator. "See here, Mason; you know those wires overhead, I'm thinking?"

"Like a book."

"On the tap of eleven I send the man on the north branch home for a good stop."

"Officially, eh?" grinned Mason.

"He'll think so, and that answers."

"And then?"

"Get aloft and cut out."

Mason started and looked serious.

"See here, Grizzly," he objected.

"Did you think I sent for you at twenty dollars a night for fun?"

"No, but----"

"It's this serious: It's a wreck, and a bad one, but if it goes through it's a thousand dollars apiece for us."

CHAPTER XIII—"HOLD THE LIMITED MAIL!"

Ralph pressed closer to his loophole of observation at the amazing announcement of Grizzly, the traitorous train dispatcher.

"A wreck, you say?" observed Mason, in a dubious and faint-hearted tone of voice.

"Oh, nobody will get hurt," declared Grizzly lightly. "What's the matter with you? Haven't you got any nerve? I said there was a thousand apiece in this, didn't I?"

"I know you did."

"So, don't weaken about the knees when I give the word, but do just as I tell you. This affair to-night is a mere flyspeck to what's coming along in a week."

"Suppose--suppose we're found out?" suggested Mason.

"We get out, isn't that all? And we get out with good friends to take care of us, don't we?"

"I suppose that's so," admitted Mason, but he shifted about in his seat as if he was a good deal disturbed.

Grizzly glanced again at the clock. Then he returned to his instrument. In a minute or two his fingers worked the key. Ralph watched and listened with all his might. What the operator did was to notify the dispatcher at Wellsville that he might go off duty, signing headquarters. Before he did this he spoke a few quick words that Ralph did not catch. Mason had selected some tools from his bag, and at once went nimbly aloft among the cable wires.

Ralph heard Mason fussing among the wires. He could only surmise what the two men were up to. The way he figured it out was that Mason had cut the wires running from the north branch through the relay into headquarters. He had thus completely blocked all messages from or to the north branch.

Mason came back to the operating room looking flustered and nervous.

"Nothing open north?" inquired Grizzly.

"Not on the Preston branch."

"That's right. We can splice 'em up again after two o'clock. Things will do their happening between now and then, and we leave no trace."

"See here, Grizzly," pleaded Mason in a spasmodic outburst of agitation; "what's the deal?"

"What good will it do you to know?"

"Well, I want to."

"All right; there's to be a runaway. There's an old junk engine down beyond Wellsville doing some dredging work, with a construction crew. She's to be fired along."

"What for?" inquired Mason, his eyes as big as saucers.

"For instance," jeered Grizzly, with a disagreeable laugh.

"Where's she to run to?"

The operator went to a map tacked to the wall. He ran his finger so rapidly over it that, the intent Mason standing between, Ralph could not clearly make out the route indicated.

"Nobody hurt, you see," remarked Grizzly, in an offhanded way. "There isn't another wheel running on that branch this side of Preston."

"No, but the feeders and cut-ins? Along near Preston the Limited mail runs twenty miles since they've been bridging the main at Finley Gap."

"She must take her chances, then," observed Grizzly coolly. "Don't get worried, son. The men working this deal know their business, and don't want to get in jail."

"What--what is there for me to do." inquired Mason, acting like a man who had been persuaded to a course that had unnerved and distressed him.

"Set those wires back just as they were, when I give you the word."

"Say, if you don't mind, I'll go somewhere and get a bracer. I'm feeling sort of squeamish."

Grizzly regarded the speaker with a contemptuous look in his manifestation of weakness, but he made no remark, and Mason left the room. Ralph from his point of observation watched him descend the stairs and close the door after him as he went out into the storm, faced in the direction of the town.

The young railroader started down the cleat ladder, when Grizzly came out of the operating room. He looked thoughtful, as if he was uneasy at his comrade wandering off. As the lower door closed after him, Ralph decided that he was bent on joining Mason in his search for "a bracer," and that now was his chance.

There flashed through the brain of Ralph the situation complete. A wreck was to happen, why and exactly where he could only guess. Clearly outlined in his mind, however, was the route ahead and beyond. By a rapid exertion of memory he could place every train on the road now making its way through the storm-laden night towards Stanley Junction. The Great Northern spread out in a quick mental picture like a map.

Ralph decided what to do, and he did not waste a second. He was down the cleat ladder and up the stairs and into the operating room in a jiffy. His thought was to give the double danger signal to headquarters and call for the immediate presence of the head operator or the chief dispatcher himself, if on duty.

It took him a minute or two to get the exact bearings of the instruments. At headquarters he was entirely familiar with the rheostat, wheat-stone bridge, polarized relays, pole changers and ground switches, but the station outfit was not so elaborate, the in table being provided only with the old relay key and sounder. His finger on the key, tapping the double danger challenge for attention, Ralph felt himself seized from behind.

With a whirl he was sent spinning across the room and came to a halt, his back against the out table, facing Grizzly. The latter had returned to the operating room suddenly and silently. His dark, scowling face was filled with suspicion.

"What's this? Aha, I know you!" spoke the operator. "How did you come here?" and he advanced to seize the intruder. Ralph read that the fellow guessed that he was trapped. There was a dangerous gleam in his eyes, and the young railroader knew that he was in a dangerous fix.

One hand of Grizzly had gone to his side coat pocket, as if in search of a weapon. His shoulders egan to crouch. He was more than a match for Ralph in strength, and the latter did not know how soon his comrade Mason might return.

Ralph was standing with his back to the operating table. He put his hands behind him, quietly facing Grizzly, and let his right hand rest on the key. Carefully he opened the key and had clicked west twice when, quick as lightning, Grizzly jumped at him.

"Stop monkeying with that instrument!" he yelled. "You spy!"

There was a struggle, and Ralph did his best to beat off his powerful and determined opponent, but he tripped across a stool and went flat on his back on the floor. The operator was upon him in a moment. His strong hands pinned Ralph's arms outspread.

"You keep quiet if you know what's healthy for you," warned Grizzly. "You're Fairbanks?"

"Yes, that is my name," acknowledged Ralph.

"And you've been watching us, and you was put up to it. Say, how much do you know and how many have you told about it?"

Ralph was silent. Just then there was a stamping up the stairs. Mason came blustering in.

"No lights ahead. I guess the stores are all shut up," he began, and intercepted himself with a stare at Ralph and a vivid:

"Hello!"

"Don't move!" ordered the telegraph operator in an irascible tone of voice. "We're in it deep, it seems. Hand over that bunch of rope near the stove, Mason."

"What are you going to do?"

"Cut for it. I know this fellow, and he isn't here for nothing. Our game's blown, or it will be. You needn't squirm," he directed at Ralph. "There's two of us now."

Ralph's hands were tied in front of him and his feet secured, as well. It was only half-heartedly, however, that Mason assisted. He was pale and scared.

"Throw him across those blamed instruments, so they will keep quiet," ordered Grizzly.

Ralph was roughly thrown upon the table, face downward, so that the relay was just under his waist. His weight against the armature stopped the clicking of the sounder. The two men grouped together in a corner, conversing rapidly and excitedly in undertones.

As luck would have it, Ralph's left hand was in such a position that it just touched the key. He opened the key and pretended to be struggling quite a little.

Grizzly came over and gave him a push in the ribs.

"You keep quiet, or I'll find a way to make you," he said, with a fierce scowl.

Ralph became passive again. As the conspirators resumed their conversation, however, he began to telegraph softly on the west main line, which was clear. His objective point was Tipton.

It was here, within the next hour, that the Limited mail would arrive and, farther on, take the Preston cut-off for twenty miles, unless stopped. The relay being shut off by his weight, there was no noise from the sounder, and he sent so slowly that the key was noiseless. Ralph did not know on whom he was breaking in, but he kept on. He told the exact state of affairs, repeated the message twice, and trusted to luck. Then his last clickings went over the wire:

"T.B.I. T.I.S.--Hold the Limited Mail. Answer quick."

CHAPTER XIV—OLD 93

The west wire was open, sure enough, and Ralph had accomplished his purpose. He knew it, and he felt a thrill of satisfaction as he heard the sharp tic-tac that announced the receipt of his message. He had raised up off the sounder.

"L. M. due at 11:53. Will hold--9," and 9, Ralph well knew, meant train orders. He had stirred up a hornet's nest for the conspirators, present and absent, and headquarters would soon get busy in running down the plot of the night.

"He's done it!" almost shrieked Grizzly, as the return message conveyed to his expert ear the sure token that Ralph had shrewdly, secretly out-rivaled him. "Did you send a message?" he yelled, jumping at Ralph, both fists raised warningly, while his eyes glared with baffled fury.

"That is what I am here for," replied the young railroader tranquilly. "You had better try and undo what you have already done."

Bang! Seizing an iron bar, the maddened operator smashed into the open west wire, as if that did any good. Then he grabbed at Ralph and threw him brutally to the floor. His foot was raised, as if to wreak a cruel vengeance upon his defenseless victim, but his companion interposed.

"See here, Grizzly," he shouted, snatching up the tool bag and making for the door, "I'm shy!"

The operator bent his head towards the instrument, now clicking away urgently and busily, growled out like a caged tiger, and ran to his desk and ripped open drawer after drawer.

Ralph watched him poke papers and other personal belongings into his pockets. With a final snarl at Ralph, he made after Mason.

"It's a big jump, and a quick one," Ralph heard him say to his hurrying companion, as they bolted down the stairs, "but a thousand dollars goes a long way."

Their footsteps faded away. Ralph was now alone. He listened intently to the messages going over the wires. O.S. messages, consists, right of track orders began to fly in every direction, while ever and constantly from headquarters came the keen imperative hail:

"R.S.--R.S.--sine."

"I've got no 'sine' and nothing to say," replied Ralph, half humorously, despite his forlorn situation. "It's wait for somebody now, and somebody will be along soon--sure enough!"

It was old Glidden who broke in upon the solitude first. He came up the outside stairs in big jumps and burst into the operating room breathless, his eyes agog.

"Hello! H'm! thought something wrong. Up with you, Fairbanks," he shouted, pulling at Ralph and tearing him free from his bonds. "Now, then, out with it, quick! What's up?"

"Foul play."

"I guessed it. The double call enlightened me, and you've got headquarters and down lines wild. Out with it, I say!"

Ralph talked about as fast as he had ever done. There was need for urgency, he felt that. The old operator knew his business.

"I'll mend up this mess," he said promptly. "That smashup--get to the superintendent. Do something anyway. Be a live wire!"

Ralph ran down from the relay room. He could trust Glidden to get at work and straighten out the tangle left behind by the fugitive conspirators.

The north branch was cut out and the operator ordered off duty. Ralph trusted to it that Glidden would try some circuitous work to get word around to the other end of the branch.

"Anyhow, the Limited is safe," ruminated Ralph, as he reached the ground.

His first thought was to get to headquarters. He looked for some stray freight or switch locomotive to help him on his way. He made out a live one on a side track. Ralph ran over to it.

"Hello, Roberts!" he hailed, recognizing the fireman, and a jolly-faced, indolent looking young fellow smiled a welcome. "Going to the Junction?"

"Exactly the other way."

Ralph, his foot on the step of the tender, drew back disappointedly.

"Waiting for Bob Evers. He's my engineer," explained Roberts. "We're to run to Acton, over the old dumping tracks--north branch."

"What!" exclaimed Ralph eagerly. "Right away?"

"No, any time; so we report at 5 a. m. for a short haul on the north branch."

"Look here, Roberts," said the young railroader eagerly, "you think I understand my business?"

"Know it, Fairbanks," nodded the fireman.

"When will Evers be here?"

"Any time within two hours."

"Two hours?" retorted Ralph. "That won't do at all. I'm going for a special order, and I want you to have steam up to the top notch by the time I get back."

"That so," drawled the fireman in his usual indolent fashion, but he arose from his lounging attitude instantly, and his great paw of a hand grasped the coal scoop with zest. "All right."

"Good for you," said Ralph, and he started back to the relay station.

"Mr. Glidden," he spoke rapidly, as he came again into the operating room. "There is no time to lose. All we know is that a wild engine is to be sent down the north branch."

"Yes, that's all we know, and no way to stop it," replied Glidden.

"There may be a way. Ninety-three is fired up for a fly down the dump to Acton."

"Aha!" nodded the old operator, pricking up his ears with interest.

"I don't say it, but it may be that we can get to the branch before the runaway does."

"Suppose so?"

"We'll set the switch and ditch her."

"Good boy!"

"I have no orders, though."

"I'll give them to you--I'll fix it up with headquarters. Fire away."

Ralph was out of the relay station and down the tracks in a hurry. Roberts was bustling about and had fired up the old switch locomotive as if ordered for a mile-a-minute dash.

"What's the programme?" he inquired simply.

"To reach the north branch just as quick as we can."

"All right. You'll run her?"

"Yes."

"You know how."

Ralph was delighted with his helper. Roberts made no delay, asked no questions. Ralph was all nerved up with the exploit in view.

Their destination was a good forty miles to the northwest. The dump tracks comprised practically an abandoned line, and, as Ralph knew, was free of either freight or passenger traffic at that hour. It was occasionally used as a cut-off in cases of emergency. The roadbed was somewhat neglected and uneven, but he had run over it twice within a few months, and as they started out Roberts announced that their special orders had shown clear tracks.

The route was a varied one, and there were some odd old-fashioned curves and a few hair-raising ten per cent. grades.

No. 93 buckled down to work right royally. There were two switches to unset, and then right again before they left the main line. At these points Roberts ran ahead and did emergency duty.

As they slid off onto the dump tracks, Ralph consulted the clock in the cab, estimated distance and set his running pace.

"She acts like a pet lamb," he observed approvingly to Roberts after a five-mile spurt.

"Yes, she'll chase to terminus all right if the coal holds out," replied the fireman. "There's a bunch of sharp curves and steep grades ahead."

"Here's one of them, see," said Ralph, and he pushed back the throttle and let the locomotive move on its own momentum.

The sturdy little engine wheezed through cuts, grunted up grades and coughed down them.

"She's only an old tub," submitted Roberts, though fondly; "but how do you like her, anyway?"

"Famous!" declared Ralph, warming to his work.

The run for a good twenty miles was a series of jarring slides, the wheels pounding the rails and straining towards a half tip over a part of the time.

There was not a signal light along the old, abandoned reach of tracks, and only one or two scattered settlements to pass. At length they came in sight of the signals of the north branch. No. 93 paralleled it on a curving slant for nearly a mile.

They were barely two hundred rods from the point where they would slide out onto the rails of the branch, and Ralph had started to let down on speed, when his helper uttered a vivid shout.

"Fairbanks--something coming!"

Ralph cast his eyes to the other side of the cab. Something, indeed, was coming--coming like a flash, going like a flash. It whizzed even with them, and ahead, like some phantom of the rail. Its course was so swift that the cab lights were a flare, then a disappearing speck.

"We are too late," said Ralph. "That is the runaway."

"So?" questioned Roberts, who only half understood the situation.

"We ran here in the hopes of ditching that engine."

"Did?"

"We're too late."

"Are?"

"Roberts," added the young railroader determinedly, "we've got to catch that runaway."

"Then it's a race, is it?" asked Roberts, grasping the fire rake.

"Yes."

"I'm with you to the finish," announced the doughty fireman of No. 93.

CHAPTER XV—CHASING A RUNAWAY

"What's the programme?" asked Roberts, after filling the fire box with coal.

"We must beat the speed of that runaway locomotive," replied Ralph.

The wild engine was going at a terrific rate of progress. Ralph could only surmise where she had been started on her mad career. The motive, her intended destination, how long she would last out--all this he could only guess at.

A drift of cinders struck his face as he shot No. 93 across a switch and out upon the in track of the north branch. At the same time he bent his ear and listened critically to the chug-chug of the escape valves.

"Some one is aboard of that engine," he told Roberts.

"Then it's a chase instead of a race," said the fireman. "All right. You boss and watch out ahead."

Pursued and pursuer were now on parallel tracks. Ralph wondered if he could be mistaken, and the locomotive ahead a special or returning from duty.

To test this he gave a familiar challenge call. From ignorance or defiance there was no response. Ralph was sure that the locomotive was in charge of some one. Its movements, the cinder drift, the wheeze of the safety valve, told that the machinery was being manipulated.

Ralph cast up in his mind all the facts and probabilities of the hairbreadth exploit in which he was participating. He acted on the belief that the locomotive he was chasing was wild, or soon to be put in action as one. It would be run to some intended point, abandoned, and sent full speed ahead on its errand of destruction.

Ralph did not know what might be ahead on either track. The schedule, he remembered, showed no moving rolling stock this side of the north main. He urged his fireman to fire up to the limit and did some rapid calculating as to the chances for the next twenty miles.

The locomotive ahead was fully a mile away before Roberts got old 93 in the right trim, as he expressed it. He clucked audibly as his pet began to snort and quiver. Pieces of the machinery rattled warningly, but that only amused him.

"She's loose-jointed," he admitted to Ralph; "but she'll hold together, I reckon, if you can only keep her to the rails. That fellow ahead is sprinting, but we're catching up fast. What's the ticket?"

"Our only hope is to beat the runaway and switch or bump her."

"There'll be some damage."

"There will probably be worse damage if we don't stop her."

The paralleled tracks widened a few miles further on to get to the solid side of a boggy reach. It was here that No. 93 came fairly abreast of the runaway. It was here, too, that the furnace door of the runaway was opened to admit coal, and the back flare of the hissing embers outlined the figure of a man in the cab.

"She's spurting," observed Roberts, watching all this, as the runaway started on a prodigious dash.

"I see she is," nodded Ralph, grimly trying to hold No. 93 over, yet aware that she was already set at her highest possible point of tension.

"And we're getting near."

"Yes, there are the station lights ahead."

About four hundred yards to the left the runaway dashed past a deserted station. Ralph never let up on speed. The chase had now led to the cut-off, a stretch of about twenty miles. Where this ran into the main again there was an important station. This point Ralph was sure had been advised of the situation from headquarters if Glidden had done his duty, and the young railroader felt sure that he had.

"Hello; now it is a chase!" exclaimed Roberts.

In circling into the cut-off No. 93 had passed a series of switches, finally sending her down the same rails taken by the runaway.

"It's now or never, and pretty quick at that," said Ralph to his fireman. "Crowd her, Roberts."

"She's doing pretty nigh her best as it is," replied the fireman. "I don't know as she'll stand much more crowding."

"That's better," said Ralph in a satisfied tone, as, fired up to the limit, the old rattletrap made a few more pounds of steam.

"Going to scare or bump the fellow ahead?" grinned Roberts, his grimed face dripping with perspiration. "We're after her close now. It's our chance to gain. They don't dare to coal up for fear of losing speed."

A score of desperate ideas as to overtaking, crippling, wrecking or getting aboard of the runaway thronged the mind of the young railroader. They were gaining now in leaps and bounds.

It was at a risk, however, Ralph realized fully. No. 93 was shaking and wobbling, at times her clattering arose to a grinding squeal of the wheels, as though she resented the terrific strain put upon her powers of speed and endurance.

"Whew! there was a tilt," whistled Roberts, as No. 93 scurried a curve where she threatened to dip clear over sideways into a swampy stretch which had undermined the solid roadbed.

Ralph gave a sudden gasp. He had watched every movement of the machinery. To his expert, careful ear every sound and quiver had conveyed a certain intelligent meaning.

Now, however, No. 93 was emitting strange noises--there was a new sound, and it boded trouble.

It came from the driving rod. Roberts caught the grinding, snapping sound, stared hard from his window, craning his neck, his eyes goggling, and then drew back towards the tender with a shout:

"Go easy, Fairbanks; something's tearing loose--look out!"

The warning came none too soon. Ralph slipped from his seat and dropped backwards into the tender just in time.

A giant steel arm had shot through the front of the cab. It was the right driving rod. It came aloft and then down, tearing a great hole in the floor. It shattered the cab to pieces with half a dozen giant strokes. It smashed against the driving wheels with a force that threatened to wreck them.

Then it tried to pound off the cylinder. The flying arms next took the roof supports, snapping them like pipe stems, and buried the fireman in a heap of debris.

"Jump!" gasped Roberts.

"I stay," breathed Ralph.

And, stripped of everything except her cylinder, No. 93 dashed on--a wreck.

CHAPTER XVI—THE WRECK

The battered locomotive continued its course for nearly half a mile, with engineer and fireman crouching back on the coal of the tender. There was a diversion of the circling driving rod as the pace slackened.

Then a violent hissing sound told of a leak somewhere in the machinery. The great steel locomotive slowed down like a crippled giant.

"She's dead," said Roberts, choking a queer sound way down in his throat. "Old 93!"

Ralph jumped to the ground and the fireman after him. The latter went all around the stalled locomotive, shaking his head mournfully.

Ralph hastened ahead out of the glare of the headlight and peered down the rails. For nearly two minutes he stood, shading his eyes with one hand to bring the disappearing runaway within focus. The wild engine had sped on its way untrammeled. He made out that she had slowed up. In the distance he fancied he saw a brisk form spring from the cab. Ralph figured it out that a switch had been set.

Then the runaway started again. He fancied that some one jumped from the cab after the engine had got in motion. He could catch the sharp clack-clack of the flying wheels ringing in the distance.

"She is running wild now," murmured the intent young railroader, and then started with a shock.

A horrid clamor extended out. It must have been a mile away, but the air was death-like, it was so still, and the merest sound seemed to vibrate clearly.

Crash, crash, crash! It sounded as if a building had collapsed against other tottering structures, tumbling them all into a mass of ruins.

"They've done it, whatever it is," said Ralph, and ran back speedily to No. 93 and Roberts. The latter stood with his ear bent in the direction of the runaway, and his usually jolly face was serious.

"What's up, Fairbanks?" he asked at once.

"A smashup, I judge," answered Ralph. "Can you dig out any lanterns?"

"Red?"

"Yes."

"Those two on the end of the tender are all right. There's another under my seat, if it hasn't got smashed."

"Run back with the two and signal both tracks," ordered Ralph. "I'm going ahead to see what has happened."

Ralph fished among the litter in the dismantled cab and found and lit the lantern referred to by Roberts. Then he started ahead down the tracks.

When he arrived at the switch he could trace that it had recently been set for a siding. A little farther on footsteps in the snow showed where some one had jumped from the runaway locomotive. Ralph paused at this spot for only a moment. He went down the siding, which curved in and out among a series of bluffs and gullies.

As he remembered it, the siding was not of great length, and ended at the side of a granite pit. A last turn brought him in full view of this. Ralph paused, a good deal wonderstruck.

Thirty feet down at the bottom of the gully lay a tangled wreckage of wood and iron. There had apparently stood two cars where the runaway had struck.

One of them held a derrick outfit, the other some heavy excavating machine. The two cars had been forced headlong into the abyss. The runaway engine piling down upon them had completed the work of ruin.

"I can't understand it," spoke Ralph, after a long spell of inspection and thought. "What possible object could any one have in view in smashing up that machinery?"

Then it occurred to him that his pursuit of the runaway might have frightened its operator from his original purpose, and he had changed his plans and abandoned the locomotive to its later course.

"A pretty bill for the Great Northern to settle, all the same," reflected Ralph, as he started back the way he had come.

At the switch he turned the target to open main, and made his way forward till he reached No. 93. Roberts had set the danger signals behind them, and he stood on the side of the embankment dismally surveying the wreck of his pet locomotive. Ralph told him of the situation ahead.

"I can't understand it," confessed the puzzled fireman.

"No more can I," said Ralph. "I wish we could have caught the man who got away, though."

"What are we going to do?"

"Wait for instructions, of course. There is nothing due out or in for some time to come, unless the Limited comes on. The out track is clear for her, if she does. We must get word to Preston, some way."

"That isn't far away," suggested Roberts.

"Too far to cover in any reasonable time. I want to get at your tool box, Roberts."

"All right."

Ralph secured a pair of pliers from the box in the cab, and went up the embankment to where the telegraph wires ran. He selected a rough pole, ascended it nimbly, and soon sat astride of the crosstrees.

The young railroader located the main service wire and began to pry it apart where there had been a splice on the insulator. When he had it separated he knew from the contact that it was in live use. Putting end to end, he began to tap off what he wanted to say.

Ralph did not know what business he might be breaking in upon. He was pretty sure that his message would be taken notice of somewhere along the line. When he had completed and repeated his message he put the end of one wire to his tongue. The vibrations were vague, but sensitive, and he knew that he had stirred up the service, and operators on the line towards headquarters were getting busy. He readjusted the wires and descended to the ground.

"Doing some stunts, aren't you?" observed Roberts, with a commending smile.

"I'm trying to get things in order," replied Ralph.

"It's you for it, every time," declared the friendly fireman. "Wish I had brains."

"Some one will be sure to come to your relief before long," said Ralph. "I have done all I can to open up the line, but I think I had better get to Preston and in direct communication with headquarters."

"It's a long trip," suggested Roberts.

"That can't be helped. I will set my red lantern half a mile ahead on the in track, for fear they don't quite understand the situation at Preston."

"So long; you're a good one," nodded Roberts approvingly.

Ralph started on his way, set the lantern and accomplished a mile without meeting with any further adventures. It was when he was about two miles on his course when that whistling in the rear caused him to halt and watch and wait.

In about five minutes the Limited whisked by, making up time. Ralph was pretty thoughtful as he followed in her trail after she had passed on.

There were a good many angles to the exploit of the night to figure out. His independent course in trying to stop the runaway might result in some censure, though he fancied not.

The identity of the wrecker and his motive were what puzzled the young railroader.

Ralph trudged on, thinking of all this, when, crossing a bridge, he peered closely over to where a light was flashed and then a second. Some one was igniting matches, apparently to light a pipe. He made out one, then two vague forms a short distance down the shore of the creek.

It was a pretty early hour of the morning for any one to be tramping around for fun. As Ralph thought of the man who had abandoned the runaway locomotive, he determined on an investigation.

He descended to the near shore, lined it, and, sharply turning a snow-laden brush heap, almost stumbled on two persons on its other side. Ralph caught his breath and drew back just in time to escape discovery.

Peering cautiously, he made out a man seated on the ground. He was groaning with pain and rubbing one limb tenderly. In front of him was a boy.

"You see, I sprained my foot crossing a broken culvert," the man said.

"Yes, yes, I see," responded his companion, and the voice thrilled Ralph, for he recognized the accents as those of a tried and true boy friend of old--Zeph Dallas.

CHAPTER XVII—A STRANGE MESSAGE

Ralph had known the time when a good many of the boys and railroad men at the Junction had considered Zeph Dallas a joke. He himself, however, had tried to take Zeph as seriously as he could, and now his erratic young friend rose still higher in his estimation.

In every live town there are generally one or more lads with the detective fever. Zeph had wandered to Stanley Junction all on fire with it. He had liked railroading, but he disdained its humdrum phases. Step by step he had kept on the trail of "detecting something," until he had unraveled a real mystery, had been of signal aid to the road detective of the Great Northern, and had practically become a hired and loyal helper to that experienced officer.

Ralph recalled the flying visit of Zeph to his mother at Stanley Junction less than ten days previous. On that occasion Zeph had dropped some mysterious and significant hints to Mrs. Fairbanks that he was "working on a big case." He had even asked her to warn Ralph "to look out for dispatching trouble."

There was no doubt in the mind of Ralph that Zeph was on the present spot on duty pure and simple. Inside of a very few minutes he was aware of the real situation of affairs. The crippled man in whose company he had found Zeph was the man who had operated the runaway engine. As Ralph peered closer he believed him to be one of the men with whom he had seen the grandfather of Glen Palmer, and whom he had later encountered in the railroad tunnel the night of the burglary of the paymaster's house.

Ralph listened attentively as the man seated on the ground began to dolefully recite a lying story of how he had got hurt. How much of this Zeph took in Ralph could not guess, for Zeph was playing a part. The man pretended to be a member of a construction gang, with friends at a little settlement a few miles distant. Acting to perfection a simple country bumpkin, Zeph pulled the wool completely over the eyes of the fellow.

"You've helped me this far," the man said, "and that makeshift crutch is a big help, but I don't think I can navigate ahead alone."

"That's all right," declared Zeph ingenuously. "If it isn't too far, I'll stay with you till you reach your friends, mister."

"Say, you're mighty obliging. I'll make it worth your while, too. I'll pay you well."

"Oh, I don't care so much for that," said Zeph. "What I'd like to do is to get settled down to some steady job."

"H'm," murmured the man reflectively, looking Zeph over in a speculative way, "I don't know but I might steer you right up against a good thing."

"I'm willing, I tell you," declared Zeph, with a rural drawl that caused Ralph to smile. "What doing, mister?"

"Just hanging around with a pleasant crowd and running some errands once in a while. There's jumps in the business pretty lively, but no real work."

"Why, I thought you was with a construction gang?"

"Um," observed the man in an embarrassed way--"yes, yes, just so. Changing my job, that's it. On my way to join certain friends on a new deal when that confounded locomotive went too fast for me, and--"

"Eh," projected Zeph. "You didn't say anything about a locomotive before, mister."

"Say, you're pretty keen, you are," chuckled the man. "And I guess you'll do. I was going to say till a locomotive loosened a log across a culvert and I stumbled over it."

"Oh, that explains it," said Zeph with a frank relief that was most fetching. "All right. You get me a job with your friends and you'll find me a good worker."

"Don't doubt it. Let's make a start."

The man winced and groaned as Zeph helped him to his feet. The latter had rigged up a forked stick so that it answered for a crutch on one side. Zeph got on the other side of the man who, leaning on his shoulder with his hand, was able to hobble along.

Ralph could foresee no particular purpose gained in keeping on the trail. He felt certain that Zeph knew his business. He had probably been watching or waiting for the conspirators right in this locality.

"It looks that way," murmured Ralph. "Anyhow, Zeph must be keeping Bob Adair advised; is perhaps acting under his direct orders. Now he is figuring for a chance to get right in with the gang. I'll follow a little further, though, as it doesn't take me much out of my course to Preston."

After a bit of progress the train wrecker and Zeph halted again. The former was getting pretty tired. Zeph cleared away some snow from a heap of old ties. The man removed his overcoat and made a pillow of it. He rested for nearly half an hour. Then he resumed his coat and they trudged along.

"Hello," exclaimed Ralph--"and good!"

He spoke the words with animation, as following up the pursuit he came to the heap of ties where the train wrecker had rested. A memorandum book lay on the snow where it had fallen from the pocket of the man's overcoat. The night light was not sufficiently strong to enable Ralph to inspect its contents. He observed, however, that it contained letters and other documents.

"I fancy it will tell something interesting when I have time to look it over," decided the young railroader.

The train wrecker and his escort finally arrived at a stretch of single rails and here they paused. This was a cut off from the main track with which Ralph was not familiar. He had an idea, however, that it connected with some coal pit or quarry in the neighborhood of Preston. In less than ten minutes after their arrival at this spot Ralph heard a rattle on the rails. A handcar propelled by two men came into view. There was quite a lengthy talk. They seemed discussing about Zeph, for Ralph saw the latter retire to a little distance. Then he was beckoned back to the three men. The crippled one was helped aboard of the handcar, Zeph joined them, and the handcar sped away.

Ralph realized that it was futile to think of following and keeping close track of them. Zeph was in their midst, accepted as a new recruit, and the young railroader felt sanguine that he would accomplish some practical results. Ralph proceeded on his way to Preston. It must have been three o'clock in the morning when he found himself not on the north branch of the road, but on a spur considerably to the east.

The light of a little station showed, and Ralph was glad to think of rest and warmth. He reached a short platform and noticed the station agent seated between the two signal windows on duty.

The man greeted the intruder with chary suspiciousness as Ralph entered the waiting room, kicking the snow off his feet. When Ralph had introduced himself, however, he stirred himself amiably, roused up the fire in the old stove, and placed a chair for him.

"I've had a bad two hours," explained the man, "and was ready for train wreckers, smash ups, or what not. A tramp routed me out of bed at home telling me the old instrument here was raising mischief. Knew something about telegraphing himself, he said, and scented trouble. I've been lively up to a few minutes ago, getting all kinds of mixed instructions about wild locomotives and trouble generally on the north cut off."

"I can tell you something about that," said Ralph, and explained a good deal that interested his companion. "Can you get me Preston?"

"Sure--want to wire?"

"It will save me a long pull through the snow."

The operator led Ralph into his little office. As he did so Ralph noticed that a piece of bagging was tacked over one of the upper sashes and the floor covered with splintered glass. He had already observed that the operator wore a bandage over one eye, but he did not just then connect affairs in his urgency to get in communication with Preston.

This he soon did. He found the operator there aware of conditions. The crude message Ralph had sent astride the telegraph pole formed the basis for advising headquarters of what was going on. The Limited was safely on her way, and a special from the Junction was now starting to take No. 93 in tow and investigate the wreck.

Ralph sent a message to Glidden, more explicitly explaining affairs. He announced that he would return to the Junction on the first train he could catch.

He was pretty well satisfied with his work of the night, for he had done his level best and he felt sure there would be some further outcome when Bob Adair's assistant reported.

"You seem to have had some trouble here," observed Ralph, with a glance at the shattered window as he left the instrument.

"Yes, and this too," said the operator, indicating his bandaged eye. "Nearly blinded."

"How is that?" inquired Ralph.

"The west freight, about an hour ago. She passes on her usual whiz. About the middle of the train some one let fly a board--a box cover. It slashed through the window, took me in the face and keeled me clear over."

"That is strange," commented Ralph. "Are you sure it was thrown?"

"What could it blow off from?"

"That's so."

"There's the identical timber," continued the operator, touching with his foot a piece of wood as they came out to the stove again. "I used half of it to mend the fire."

Ralph picked up the piece of wood out of curiosity. As he did so he made a discovery.

Its smooth side, though blurred, bore some faint black marks like letters and words. It looked as if scratched with a blunt cinder on the ends of burned matches.

In breaking the wood to mend the fire the operator had split the piece transversely removing a part of a written line, but to his amazement Ralph could make out these words:

"Send word to Ralph Fairbanks, Stanley Junction, that Glen Palmer is--"

The remainder of this queer message was missing--ashes in the depot stove. What had been the writing complete, and what did it mean?

CHAPTER XVIII—THE SLUMP "SECRET"

"Wake up, Ralph."

The young dispatcher of Stanley Junction jumped out of bed in a bound. He felt that he could have slept half a dozen hours longer, but to every railroad man the call "wake up" means duty waits, no delay, and Ralph responded to the urgent call without hesitation.

The echo of a series of light tappings on the door and of his mother's voice mingled with her departing footsteps. He called out:

"What is it, mother?"

"A telephone message from the superintendent."

"Good--something is stirring," reflected Ralph, and hurried his dressing. "Well, enough has happened since yesterday to interest the president of the road himself," he went on, musing. "They wanted some house cleaning done, and it has begun in a vigorous way."

It was early in the afternoon. Just after daybreak that morning Ralph had reached Stanley Junction on top of a freight car. He had found Glidden in charge of the situation at the relay station.

"You've hit the mark, Fairbanks," were his first commendatory words. "The assistant superintendent was here for an hour with me after we got that rough and tumble message from you down the line."

"It was a cross tree experiment. Wasn't it a jumble?" inquired Ralph.

"We pieced it out, got our bearings, and they're spreading the net to catch some pretty big fish."

"What of Grizzly and that fellow with him?"

"Sloped. Adair is after them, though. See here, you get right home and into your cozy."

"But I have something of possible importance to tell the superintendent."

"He's gone down the line hot-footed. It will all keep till he calls you up. Left instructions to that effect--'30,' now, and be quick about it!"

"30" it was, perforce. Ralph had gone through a rough night of it. He was pretty well tired out and glad to get to bed. He went there, however, with some exciting thoughts in his mind.

There had been no solution to the enigma of the piece of broken box cover flung from the passing freight train through the window of the little station. All Ralph could do about that incident was to conjecture blindly.

It was a queer happening, a suggestive one. Ralph had a fertile imagination. There was a coincidence about the discovery of the queer message, and things hinged together in a way. Contiguous to that section the chicken farm was located, and Glen Palmer, at least his grandfather, had seemingly linked up with the conspirators against the welfare of the Great Northern road once or twice before. Ralph could not conceive why that message had been written. It was a new mystery, but it had come so secretly upon the heels of a bigger and more important one, that there was neither time nor opportunity to explore it just at present.

Mrs. Fairbanks, like the true anxious mother that she was, greeted Ralph on his arrival at home. She had not gone to bed all night, and she now insisted on his eating an early breakfast and taking a needed rest. Tired out as he was, however, once alone in his own room Ralph took this, the first quiet opportunity, to look over the memorandum book that had fallen from the coat pocket of the train wrecker.

Ralph's eyes expanded and he uttered one or two subdued whistles of astonishment as he delved among the contents of his find. Some penciled notes and a letter in the memorandum book told a great deal--in fact, so much and so clearly and unmistakably, that Ralph could hardly go to sleep thinking over the importance of his discoveries.

They had to wait, however, till he could again see the superintendent. Now, as Ralph was roused up out of sleep by a telephone call from that very official, his active mind was again filled with the theme of the memorandum book and what it had revealed to him.

When he got down stairs Ralph found that word had come for him to report to the office of the road as promptly as possible. His mother had an appetizing lunch spread on the dining room table, and the lad did full justice to it.

He was thoughtful and busy formulating in his mind just what he would report at headquarters, and had proceeded less than half a dozen squares from home when passing an alley his name was called. Looking beyond the street Ralph recognized Ike Slump. He wore a very mysterious face and he was urgently beckoning to Ralph. The latter was about to proceed on his way with a gesture of annoyance, when Slump shouted out:

"You'll be sorry if you don't see me for a minute or two."

"Well, what is it?" inquired Ralph, moving a few feet towards his challenger.

"I need five dollars."

"Oh, you do?"

"Yes, bad. I want you to give it to me."

"That's cool."

"I've got to get out of town. You'd better let me go."

"I don't see how I am preventing you," said Ralph.

"You will, when I explain."

"Then be quick about it. I have no time to waste."

"Neither have I," remarked Slump, with an uneasy glance towards the street. "To be short and sweet, I know Glen Palmer."

Ralph started a trifle at this. Slump spoke the name with a knowing look in his eyes and a sidelong leer that was sinister.

"Well, what of it?" demanded Ralph.

"I thought I'd seen him before the day I met him up at the yards. I racked my brain to recall him. This morning it all came to me."

"What do you suppose I care about your knowing him?" inquired Ralph.

"Just this: he's a friend of yours, a sort of pet. I understand you started him in the chicken farming business, so you must have some interest in him. All right, I can snip him out of his position of glory double quick," asserted Ike, in a malevolent and threatening way.

"Go ahead, what are you driving at?" asked Ralph as calmly as he could.

"Five dollars--that's what it will cost you to keep your friend from being exposed. Five dollars, and I bury the secret fathoms deep."

"In other words," said Ralph, trying hard to suppress his feelings, "you want to blackmail me?"

"Oh, no," assented Slump, "I simply want to sell this photograph," and he drew a card from his pocket. "I went to heaps of trouble to get it. It shows that I did see Glen Palmer before. It was where we were both locked up in jail," shamelessly confessed Slump.

Ralph was a good deal taken aback. The words of Slump and the photograph he extended rather took the young railroader's breath away. The portrait was that of a boy dressed in a convict suit, a number on his cap, and the background showed the surroundings of a prison room.

"It's too bad," spoke Ralph involuntarily. He was thinking of his misplaced trust in the Palmer boy. All his dark suspicions concerning the old grandfather and the conspirators were instantly revived in the mind of Ralph.

"Ain't it, though?" smirked Slump. "Is it worth the price?"

"No!" suddenly shouted Ralph, in a tone so stern and ringing that the discomfited Slump fell back several feet. "You miserable jail bird and swindler, I wouldn't help you on your wretched career of crime for five cents let alone five dollars. Furthermore, Glen Palmer may have been in jail, but I won't believe he belonged there till I have the proofs."

"Oh, won't you?" sneered Ike. "All right. Don't want to reform him, eh? Won't give the downtrodden and oppressed a chance. You're a heavy philanthropist, you are, Mr. Ralph--let go!"

Slump took a sudden whirl. From behind a fence there suddenly pounced down upon him a towering form. Ralph was as much surprised as Slump to recognize Bob Adair, the road detective.

The diligent officer gave Slump one or two more whirls, holding on to his coat collar, that made him shriek with affright. Then he threw him reeling ten feet away.

"I gave you two hours to get out of town this morning," he observed. "Now then it's two minutes to head straight for the limits, or I'll lock you up as a vagrant."

Ike picked up his fallen cap on the run. He darted down the alley in a flash.

"I don't know but what I would have liked to find out something more from him," remarked Ralph.

"Oh, I overheard the subject of your conversation," said Adair--"about that missing boy, Glen Palmer, I suppose you mean?"

"Missing--is he missing, Mr. Adair?"

"Since the day after you told me about him, and his grandfather and the queer company he kept," replied Adair. "I went down to the chicken farm to find that young Palmer had sold it out to a neighbor for a song and had vanished."

"Why, that is queer," commented Ralph. "I fancied he had got a new lease of life when I started him in business."

"Decidedly mysterious, the whole affair," added the road detective. "That will all come out when we see the superintendent. We're both due at his office."

"I was just going there," said Ralph.

"And I was on my way to meet you," explained Adair.

They walked on together for a short distance. Suddenly Adair drew out a bulky pocket book well stuffed with papers. He selected a folded yellow sheet.

"Here's something that belongs to you," he said. "There's a good deal to go over, so get that off our minds. Glidden handed it to me this noon."

"What is it?" asked Ralph.

"A telegram."

"So it is. Why--"

Ralph paused there. If he had been astonished at the discovery of the board message back at the little station, the present scrap of paper doubly mystified him.

It was the mere fragment of a telegram, no heading, no date, and it read:

"Advise Ralph Fairbanks, Stanley Junction. Look out for the pacer."

CHAPTER XIX—ON THE LOOKOUT

Ten minutes later Ralph and Bob Adair entered the office of the superintendent of the Great Northern. As they did so, a tall, well-dressed man left by another door. Adair nudged Ralph.

"The President of the road," he spoke in a low quick tone.

"Yes, I see," nodded Ralph.

"Eyes and ears wide open. We're going to see some lively doings, if I don't mistake my cue."

Ralph felt the dignity and force of the occasion. It was a good deal for a mere youth to realize that he was being called into an important conference on a footing with old and experienced railroaders. The serious yet pleasant greeting of the superintendent told that the situation was a distinct compliment to the fine record and ability of the young railroader.

Ralph modestly took a chair to one side of the big table at which the superintendent and his assistant were seated. Adair produced that formidable memorandum book of his, stuffed with all kinds of secrets of the rail.

"We had better get down to business without any preamble," spoke the head official briskly. "Before we begin, however, I wish to commend you, Fairbanks, for your diligence in our behalf."

"Thank you, sir," said Ralph with a flush of pleasure.

"Yourself and Glidden handled the situation at the relay just as we would have wished it done. What is your report, Adair?"

The road detective consulted his notes in a matter-of-fact way, and began detailing his information as if he was reading off a freight schedule, but Ralph was immensely interested and so were his other auditors.

Part of what Adair told was news to Ralph. The most of Adair's disclosures, however, linked to what he already suspected or knew. Briefly narrated, the two queerly-acting men who had been noticed by Ralph in the company of Glen Palmer's grandfather and during the trouble in the tunnel had been the starting clews in the case.

"There is a man named Rivers and half a dozen fellow conspirators who are making most of the trouble," said the road officer. "Two of the men Fairbanks spotted over two weeks ago. They were after the secrets of our paymaster, as we well know. From word I have received from an assistant, Dallas, they and a group of helpers are hanging around the vicinity of scene of the smash up last night."

"There's a mystery to explain, Adair," here broke in the superintendent. "What was the motive for the collision?"

"Just malicious mischief, I presume--a part of the contract of the gang to hamper and cripple the Great Northern all they can," returned the assistant. "The work was done by the same group--the word I have received from young Dallas assures me of that."

"If I may be allowed to say a word," submitted Ralph.

"Certainly," nodded the superintendent, and all eyes were instantly fixed on Ralph. The latter took from his pocket the memorandum book and letters which had belonged to the injured train wrecker. He explained how he had found them. There was sharp attention, while the officers expressed approval in their looks.

"From all I can gather from these," explained Ralph, "the man who ran away with the old engine was Rivers. This book bears his name. From it I would think he was receiving a goodly sum each week from some mysterious source for 'looking after' the Great Northern, as it is expressed."

"This is the underhand work of our rivals in business," declared the assistant superintendent bitterly.

"I think so, too," assented Ralph. "Outside of that, however, it is certain that Rivers and his fellow conspirators are doing some business 'on the side,' as he again aptly expresses it in his notes. A letter will show you that a man named Kingston hired him to wreck the two cars near the quarry."

"Kingston, the contractor? Why, it was his own machinery. He had a large contract to do some extensive blasting work for the Great Northern," spoke Adair.

"Yes," nodded Ralph, "I guess that from what the memorandum book tells me. The contract, however, had to be done in a certain time or Kingston forfeited a heavy bond, I believe."

"That is true," said the superintendent.

"He found out that his machinery would not do the work and that he would lose on his contract."

"And wrecked his own plant!" exclaimed the assistant superintendent.

"Incredible!" murmured the head official at his side.

"You deserve something for ferreting that out," declared Adair approbatively. "There is your evidence, gentlemen, it seems," he added, pushing the documents over to the others.

"This is getting pretty serious," observed the superintendent.

"I will hunt up the contractor," said Adair, making a note. "I have men looking for Grizzly and Mason. The other suspects in the service are being shadowed. I think, with the start this famous young friend of ours, Fairbanks, has given us, there will be a general clearing up of the situation in a short time. Dallas is in the company and confidence of the conspirators. There will be some arrests and confessions within a few days. I think I can safely promise that."

Ralph listened attentively while the others engaged in a general discussion of the situation. It was arranged that he should resume his position at headquarters in the office of the chief train dispatcher. Adair was to go down the line for the avowed purpose of getting more closely in touch with his faithful young assistant, Zeph Dallas. The latter, through the exercise of a keen intelligence and perseverance, seemed to proudly hold the key to the entire situation, and Ralph was glad of it.

"There is one other subject of importance," remarked the road officer, as the superintendent arose and the conference seemed as on end.

"What is that?"

"The pay car affair."

"I thought that was all arranged."

"It is, so far as we are concerned, but shall I advise Fairbanks of the arrangements?"

"By all means," directed the superintendent promptly.

"Yes, he has proven his trustworthiness and ability," supplemented the assistant, "and it is our wish that he should be appraised of exactly what is going on."

"Very well," nodded Adair, in his usual brusque manner, "I will attend to that. Come on, Fairbanks."

Ralph bowed courteously to his two official friends and left the room with the road officer. As they reached the street Adair linked his arm in that of Ralph in a confidential way.

"See here, Fairbanks," he remarked, "such tricks as that smash up and the pay car business any road may have to tackle from time to time. We shall attend to the fellows behind those schemes all right, but it's bigger game we are after. A plot has crippled our service, corrupted our operators, stolen our private wire information. Bear this in view, and when new things come up along that line, which they are bound to do, dig out all you can under the surface that will give us a handle against the real plotter--the rival road that is trying to throw us down."

"I understand, Mr. Adair," said Ralph.

"You are going up to the train dispatcher's office?"

"Yes."

"I'll join you there in about half an hour, as I have some cypher messages I want you particularly to attend to. I'll tell you then about this pay car business."

Ralph had to be content with this. As he walked along he wondered what Adair would have to tell him. The fifteenth of the month was only ten days ahead, and the pay car according to usual schedule should start on the regular trip three days earlier.

Ralph was glad to get back to duty pure and simple. Seated at his desk he was soon absorbed in getting accumulated work out of the way. He was pretty busy when one of the second trick men came up to him.

"Mr. Fairbanks," he said, "I thought I would speak to you about a message I took over the commercial wire early this morning."

"Is that it." inquired Ralph, at once guessing the allusion, and producing the little yellow slip of paper that the road officer had given him.

"'From Glen Palmer,'" read the operator over Ralph's shoulder--"yes, that's the one: 'Look out for the pacer.' It came in on a jumble of stuff like a quick cut in. There was more, but I couldn't catch it. I signaled 'repeat,' but lost the sine, and it was clicked so thunderingly fast I got mixed on the letters."

"You don't know the point of sending, then?" asked Ralph.

"No. I didn't know what the other end was trying to give me: Look out for the packer? faker, pacer?"

"Hello!" said Ralph, so strangely and suddenly that the operator started at him agape.

"What's the matter?" inquired the latter, wonderingly.

Ralph did not reply. He was thinking hard. A sudden light had illuminated his mind.

"I've got it," he breathed in some mental triumph. "'Look out for the pay car!'"

CHAPTER XX—A TRUSTY FRIEND

"Understand, Fairbanks?"

"Perfectly, Mr. Adair."

"The pay car goes through on regular schedule out of Stanley Junction."

"Yes, sir."

"With enough ammunition ahead to settle the hash of any possible meddlers. We'll make the test. Then the other end. A split up at the end of each section, and if the gang get ahead of us on that arrangement, they are cleverer than I thought they were."

All this would have been Greek to a person not acquainted with the facts of the case. The colloquy terminated a whispered confidential talk between Ralph and Bob Adair in the chief dispatcher's office. The road officer seemed to throw the pay car off his mind after a statement that Ralph was one of six persons who knew what was about to happen, namely, the President and superintendent of the road, the assistant superintendent, the paymaster and Adair himself.

"There will be something to keep track of Tuesday night," observed Adair. "You've got your instructions for that occasion."

"Yes, well in mind," said Ralph. "One moment before you go, Mr. Adair. I have told you about the 'pacer' message."

"Yes," nodded the road officer, "and your explanation looks plausible."

"I don't want to judge from appearances. You see, I feel like giving Glen Palmer a show."

"That's fair enough, Fairbanks. I can't help thinking, though, that he or his grandfather have had some dealings with the crowd we are after."

"It is only a theory," persisted Ralph, "but I figure it out that the old man, Glen's grandfather, is some veteran telegrapher. He isn't right in his mind, and perhaps, without Glen knowing it, he was approached secretly by the conspirators. Perhaps they have benefited from his knowledge of telegraphy in tapping the wires."

"You say the boy, too, is an expert operator?"

"From what I learn, yes," answered Ralph. "His grandfather would naturally teach him."

Adair shrugged his shoulders. It was evident he considered circumstances against the Palmers, for he said:

"I don't like their sudden disappearance. I don't fancy, either, what Slump remarked about young Palmer being a jail bird."

"That looks bad enough," admitted Ralph, "but please consider that message on the piece of board thrown through the window of the station."

"Well?"

"Didn't that show that Glen Palmer was trying to get some word to me?"

"Maybe."

"Under difficulties, too. I believe that he was a prisoner, perhaps shut into some freight car, but managing to send adrift that word to me."

"You're pretty loyal to anyone you like, Fairbanks."

"I want to do the poor fellow justice," responded Ralph. "Then later, that fragment of message 'Look out for the pay car.' I can't help thinking that the boy is straight, and wants to warn and help us."

"Hope so," said Adair brusquely. "A short time will tell. I shall soon round up the crowd, and if young Palmer is in wrong with them I shall find it out."

It seemed like getting down to a decidedly humdrum existence, routine duty at the dispatcher's desk after the exciting experience preceding. When Glidden came on duty he merely smiled in his grim way, with the words to Ralph:

"In harness again, eh? I reckon things will smooth down now."

Ralph hoped so. He believed it, too, as a few days went by and in the keen zest and interest of his new work he partially forgot the active issues of the conspiracy, which seemed to have been checked or subdued.

With the departure of Grizzly and Mason the suspicious and treacherous element seemed to be eliminated from the main office. The tricks of the enemy and their methods were now known to the dispatching force, and they were constantly on their guard. A new private code was adopted by Ralph, and a system of checking up through repeats that pretty well safeguarded them against crooked messages.

Mrs. Fairbanks was congratulating herself that affairs had quieted down permanently and was enjoying the days that brought Ralph home for the evening each day, when a new ripple on the surface of affairs set things in vivid action again.

Ralph had come home to dinner and was spending a few minutes in casual conversation with his mother after the meal, when the door bell rang sharply. Ralph answered the summons to find Glidden standing outside, his face pale and anxious, and so nervous over something that he could not stand still in the same position for a single minute.

"Any trouble, Mr. Glidden?" inquired Ralph quickly.

"Only of my own," responded the old operator. "See here, I want you to do something for me. It's a hurry business. Just tell your mother not to worry if you are away to-night."

"Is there a probability that I will be?" inquired Ralph.

"If you consent to do me the favor of my life, yes," declared Glidden quickly. "See here, I've fixed everything."

The operator shoved a slip of paper towards Ralph. It was a brief permission for Ralph to go off for twenty-four hours.

"I had to act quick," explained Glidden, "so I got that end of it fixed directly."

"I hardly understand, Mr. Glidden."

The old operator glanced at his watch and grabbed the arm of his companion.

"Come on," he insisted. "There's no time to lose. We can talk as we walk along. I don't want to bother you with my family troubles, Fairbanks, but I need a reliable friend."

"I am certainly at your service."

"Thanks. It's your way, you can't help it," commented the erratic operator. "Here's the situation: I have a brother in business at Derby."

"That's seventy-five miles down the line."

"Exactly. It seems that he owns a new mill. I don't know exactly what he does, but it's in the metal manufacturing line. He has invented a process for making a substitute for Babbitt metal."

"They use some of it at the shops, I remember," said Ralph.

"A man named Dorsett, who was his partner, started in the same line after selling out and contracting not to do so. His process is no good, and he wants to get my brother to a point where he will treat with him."

"I see," nodded Ralph, much interested.

"It seems that my brother in starting in for himself had to run in debt for his principal machinery. His old partner managed somehow to buy the debt from the machinery people. He has put the screws to my brother, got out an execution for four thousand dollars against him, and unless that amount and the costs of the judgment are paid by tomorrow, he takes possession, and my brother loses everything."

"There's lots of mean work in the world, and this is one of the hard cases," observed Ralph.

"The worst of it is," continued Glidden, "my brother never let me know about the tight fix he was in. I never should have heard of it if he had not got sick in bed. He could do no business and his lawyer wrote to me. I got the letter only an hour ago. You see how fast I must work. I've got to raise that four thousand dollars before court time tomorrow."

"Four thousand dollars?" repeated Ralph seriously--"that's a big sum of money, Mr. Glidden."

"Yes, for a poor man like me, but brother John shall have it. I can't see a good twenty thousand dollar investment wrecked to satisfy the malice of an enemy. See here--take that," and Glidden extended a package and Ralph regarded it wonderingly.

"What is it, Mr. Glidden?" he inquired.

"One thousand dollars--five years' savings, I just drew it from the bank here. I want you to take the three o'clock train for Derby. Go to my brother's lawyer, whose address I will give you. Pay him that one thousand dollars, and see if he can't use it to stave off proceedings until I get on hand bright and early tomorrow morning with the balance of the money."

CHAPTER XXI—A DASTARDLY PLOT

Ralph was greatly interested in the affairs of the Gliddens. The old dispatcher was a good fellow all around; he had proven himself a loyal friend to the young railroader, and Ralph could not resist the compliment implied in entrusting him with an important mission.

"Sure the leave of absence is all right?" he suggested.

"Saw the superintendent himself."

"Very well, I'm glad to go for you," said Ralph, and he stowed the one thousand dollars in a safe inside pocket. "How are you going to raise the other three thousand dollars, though?"

"I have a sister living at Wilston, who I know has as much as I had in bank. I'm going to take the express for there, jump to Myron, where a brother-in-law runs a small country bank, and I'm not afraid of results. My sister owns a two thousand dollar mortgage that I have an interest in, too. I'll take that on to the bank to put up as security, if it's needed."

"You're a pretty good brother, Mr. Glidden," said Ralph earnestly.

The old operator mumbled in his throat and turned away to hide the emotion that lay under his gruff manner.

By the time they reached the depot Glidden had given Ralph final detailed instructions. He did not know how his messenger might find affairs at Derby, but he seemed to take a good deal of comfort in believing that if they were at all complicated, Ralph's dexterity and intelligence would simplify the problem.

"Tell the lawyer I will be certain to reach Derby on the first morning train with the money," declared Glidden. "Stay with him all night and watch things. Keep your eye on the other crowd and guard the factory."

"I shall try to do all you suggest," promised Ralph.

He telephoned to his mother at home. It was a three hours' ride to Derby. Ralph reached his destination about five o'clock in the afternoon. He went to the office of the lawyer, located above a store, but found its door locked. Then he inquired in the place below as to his residence and received the necessary directions.

As Ralph left the store he noticed a crowd of four men lounging in front of a drinking place across the street. From their manner he judged that they had watched him go up to the office of the lawyer. Why they were interested Ralph did not know, but he kept a keen eye out, remembering that he carried a thousand dollars in an inner pocket of his coat.

"Two of those men are following me," Ralph said to himself with conviction, a minute later.

This he believed to be true, judging from their actions. They kept pace with him on the opposite side of the street. Ralph gave no sign that he suspected their surveillance. Suddenly as the two men were crossing the street, a lank, wretched looking fellow came towards them from the doorway of a saloon. It was apparent that he knew them and made some appeal to them. One of them brushed him carelessly aside. As the other passed him the mendicant caught his sleeve to detain him. The man turned, jerked away, shot out his fist, and striking the other brutally in the face sent him prostrate to the pavement and walked coolly on.

"Poor fellow!" commented Ralph, as the man picked himself up, wiping the blood from his injured face with an old ragged handkerchief.

"That's the way you treat an old friend after getting all you can out of him, is it?" shrieked the injured man, waving his fists wildly after his assailant. "I'll fix you for this. I'll get even with you."

The incident passed out of Ralph's mind as he sought for and found the home of the lawyer. As he entered its gate he glanced back down the street. The two men who had followed him stood at the next corner. Soon they turned and retraced the way they had come. Apparently they were satisfied in the proceedings, their mission having been to locate Ralph's destination.

Ralph found the wife of the lawyer at home. It took only a few minutes for a bright businesslike boy and a woman who interested herself in her husband's professional duties to understand one another. Ralph explained the object of his call.

"I am very glad to welcome you," said the lady. "And I am glad of the good news you bring. My husband and I are deeply interested in Mr. Glidden's business affairs. My husband had an urgent professional call to the next town, but he will be back at eight o'clock this evening. He was preparing to arrange for some kind of a bond tomorrow morning, but it looked dubious. The money will settle everything."

Ralph noticed a small safe in the room where he sat, and turned the thousand dollars over to the lawyer's wife for safe keeping.

"That is better so," said the lady. "Dorsett, the man who is making all this trouble, has employed three or four rough loafers in his service, and they have been watching every move my husband has made."

"I think two of them followed me here," explained Ralph.

"I hope you will watch out for yourself," warned the lawyer's wife anxiously. "Perhaps you had better remain here until my husband returns."

"Oh, I am not a bit afraid," said Ralph. "I want to look around town and perhaps go as far as the factory. Is it in operation?"

"No, it has been shut down since Mr. Glidden's illness, but it is in charge of a faithful, honest old fellow, his foreman, a man named Bartlett."

Ralph left the lawyer's house and started in the direction of the factory as just indicated to him. It appeared to be located on the river, about half a mile from the center of the town.

In order to reach it he had to go back a few blocks towards the village. He saw no trace of the men who had followed him. As he passed an alley opening, however, he slowed up to watch the maneuvers of a man who interested him.

This was the man who had been knocked over in the street by the two men who had followed Ralph. He was standing near a barrel which seemed to be used as a receptacle for the kitchen refuse of a house near by. He had reached into it and picked out a piece of stale bread and lifted it to his lips.

"Don't eat that," said Ralph impulsively, slipping quickly to the side of the man.

The latter flushed up, put the scrap of food behind him and looked rather annoyed and angry. He did not have a good face, and it looked the worse because of his recent beating. Still, the man's forlorn wretchedness appealed to the whole-hearted young railroader in a forcible way.

"What will I eat?" growled the man, scowling hard.

"You seem to be hungry--go and get a good meal somewhere."

Ralph extended half a dollar. The man stared at it, then at Ralph.

"Crackey!" he said breathlessly--"do you mean it?"

"You had better go somewhere and wash the blood off your face first," continued Ralph. "Here," and he took out the little surgical case that all locomotive men carry with them. "Put a piece of that sticking plaster on that cut across your cheekbone. It was a pretty bad blow that fellow gave you."

"Did you see him strike me?" inquired the man.

"Yes, and it appeared to be a brutal and uncalled for assault."

"Say, that's just what it was," declared the man, getting excited. "I trained with that crowd and did their dirty work, and because I got a drop too much and blowed about the things we were going to do up to the factory, they dropped me."

"What factory?" pressed Ralph.

"Glidden's."

"I was just going up there," said Ralph. "It's somewhere in this direction, isn't it?"

"You'll see the smokestack when you turn the next corner. Say," demanded the fellow with a stare of interest at Ralph, "what you going there for? Looking for a job?"

"No," replied Ralph, "I wanted to see it, that's all. I am a friend of the man who owns it."

"Oh, that's it?" observed the man thoughtfully. "Well, he won't own it tomorrow."

"Why not?"

"Dorsett is going to get him, that's why."

"You mean seize on the factory, don't you?" inquired Ralph.

The man stared at Ralph fixedly. He was silent for nearly two minutes. He seemed to be turning something over in his mind. He gazed at the coin Ralph had given him. Then he glanced over his shoulder to see if any lurker was watching them.

"See here," he asked in a low tone, "you're on Glidden's side, of course?"

"Yes, strongly."

"You've been good to me. Saved me from starving. I'll do something for you. Between twelve and one o'clock tomorrow morning, Dorsett and his men are going to pull that factory up yonder to pieces."

CHAPTER XXII—HOLDING THE FORT

Ralph was a good deal startled at the statement of the man whom he had helped to some advantage, it seemed. He did not, however, show it. The man was grateful to him, and Ralph counted on his relating something further.

"I would be glad to have you tell me a little more about this business," he said. "As I told you, I am a good deal interested in the welfare of Mr. Glidden."

"Are, eh?" grinned the man. "So was I--in the wrong way. Just now it doesn't matter one way or the other. The crowd Dorsett was working with has set me adrift, and I've got nothing to expect from them. What is it you want to know, guv'nor?"

"Just this," answered Ralph--"any tricks they are up to that aren't square."

"Lots of those, guv'nor. Dorsett is bound to break up Glidden, if he can."

"I know that; I understand he has bought up a big claim against Mr. Glidden and will put it into execution tomorrow if it isn't paid."

"That's right."

"And it will put Mr. Glidden to a lot of costs to redeem his plant."

"Say, guv'nor," here interrupted the man--"there'll be no redeeming in the case."

"Why not?"

"Because the money isn't what Dorsett is after. He's got lots of that. He simply wants to squeeze Glidden so close that he'll holler and quit. He's bent on rooting out the plant entire. Then when he's got Glidden down in the mud, he expects he'll sell him his secret chemical process for a mere song."

"The scoundrel!" exclaimed Ralph hotly.

"I knew that long ago," coolly chuckled the fellow. "If you're interested, let me give you a tip."

"I shall be thankful."

"Get the lawyer to have some one stay all night at the plant."

"There's the foreman, Bartlett, I understand."

"Yes, day times. You do as I say."

"I'll stay myself."

"That might do. You are interested, aren't you, mightily? Then so am I. Say, inasmuch as I've blabbed a part of it, out with the whole, say I. There's going to be a raid on the factory, as I hinted to you, just after midnight."

"A raid?"

"Exactly. To-morrow the time for Glidden to put up a bond or pay the four thousand dollars expires."

"Yes," replied Ralph, "and by ten o'clock, court time, it will be paid."

"Too late."

"Eh?"

"Hours too late--nigh on to half a day too late."

"Why do you say that?"

"Because it's a fact."

"In what way?"

The man screwed his eyes up shrewdly as if he enjoyed making a clever disclosure. Then he said:

"Dorsett has made an arrangement with a drunken justice of the peace in the next township to open office at one minute after twelve, midnight. The justice will issue an execution. Inside of an hour Dorsett and his men will be at the factory. They don't have to wait for court time. They intend to levy on the machinery only. They won't put a custodian in charge nor wait for redemption nor anything else. They'll simply rip out all those valuable tank machines and piping that cost a fortune, bid the plunder in at old junk prices and gobble up everything else before Glidden or his lawyer are awake and out of bed."

"My man," spoke Ralph rapidly, and moved to indignation and excitement almost beyond control, "are you sure of what you say?"

"As I was, up to this morning, one of the men who was to help in wrecking the plant, I reckon I know what I'm talking about," answered the man.

"I will pay you to take me up to the plant," said Ralph, "as quickly as you can."

"You'll pay me nothing," replied the other. "You needn't be afraid of any trouble until midnight. Dorsett is too keen to overslip the law in any way. His men may hang around and dog your footsteps and spy about and all that, but they'll do no harm until Dorsett has the power right in his hands. Then--look out."

"Yes, indeed," said Ralph reflectively.

His guide went with him until they came to the factory. Here he left Ralph, saying he was almost starved and must get a good meal.

The factory was a grim-looking, isolated, one-story stone building. One end was rounded with brick and had heavy iron shutters. The front was a kind of office. Behind it was an iron partition and a windowless stretch of factory room fully fifty feet in length.

Ralph tried the front door and found it locked. In a minute or two, however, a big, stalwart man with a face of considerable character came from the inner room. He did not open the door, but stood at a window and called out:

"What do you want?"

"Are you Mr. Bartlett?" inquired Ralph.

"That's me."

"I am a friend to Mr. Glidden, and I come here from his lawyer."

"Where's the proof of it? I don't know you," said Bartlett guardedly.

"That's so," said Ralph, "and I am glad to find you so particular. My name is Fairbanks, and I come from the brother of Mr. Glidden, at Stanley Junction. I have a good deal to tell you, and wish you would come out and talk with me or let me in to talk to you."

"You say the lawyer knows you?" inquired Bartlett warily.

"No, he doesn't, but his wife does."

"We'll see about that--wait a minute."

Ralph was made aware of the fact that the factory connected with the town by telephone, as the foreman of the plant proceeded to an instrument and took down the receiver. He could not hear the conversation that ensued, but very shortly Bartlett came to the door and invited him in.

"You're all right, and you're bringing some mighty good news, I hear," he said heartily. "Sit down. I fancy that blatherskite, Dorsett, won't sail so high tomorrow."

"I fancy not, if things are done straight," said Ralph, "but I just learned something that worries me a good deal."

"What is that?"

Ralph told his story in detail. He recited what his tramp acquaintance had imparted to him. The sturdy foreman knit his brows, but he did not scare a bit. He walked slowly over to a closet, took out a new Winchester rifle, laid it across the top of the desk, and said quietly:

"I've got orders to admit no one here without an order from the lawyer up to ten o'clock tomorrow morning. The man who gets in before that time on any other conditions will be a dandy, I can tell you that."

Ralph requested permission to use the telephone. He got in communication with the lawyer's wife and told her of his new discoveries. Her husband had not yet returned, but as soon as he appeared she told Ralph she would send him up to the plant. Ralph informed her that he would not leave the factory until he heard from the lawyer.

It was getting dusk when a small boy came to the office door. He carried a basket and a note, which, after due challenge, Bartlett took into his possession. The lawyer's wife had sent them a steaming hot supper, and told Ralph in the note to hold the fort, as she felt certain that her husband would arrive at Derby on either the eight or ten o'clock train.

Half an hour later, after they had lighted up, the foreman approached the door cautiously as some one else knocked at it.

"Who's there?" he demanded.

"No one you know. The young fellow in there knows me, though. Tell him to look out of the window."

Ralph pulled aside the shade and peered out, recognizing his tramp acquaintance of the afternoon.

"It's the man who told me about this plot of Dorsett's," he said.

"One of the same gang, eh? I dunno," remarked Bartlett dubiously. "Ain't he a dangerous customer to let inside here?"

"He seems friendly, and he may have something more to tell us," responded Ralph. "I hardly think we'll take much risk admitting him."

"Well, it's just as you say, then."

"Yes, let him in," directed Ralph.

He regarded his tramp friend with some surprise and curiosity as the foreman admitted him. The man had got a clean shave and his face patched up, and apparently had a very satisfactory meal inside of him, for he was blandly cheerful and complacent.

"Saw three of our friends on my way here," he said to Ralph.

"You mean Dorsett's friends?"

"Yes. Two of them were down by the turnpike, probably watching to see if the lawyer or others might come here. The other fellow I spied hanging around the furnace room. He was on the roof once, but he just sneaked away."

"What did you come here for?" inquired Bartlett bluntly.

"Oh, I took a kind of fancy to this young fellow. He did me a kind turn, and I'd like to return the compliment. Thought maybe there might be a ruction later, and if there is, I'm on your side. So count on me."

With a grin and chuckle the speaker bunched up a fist that resembled a huge knot of mahogany.

"I think I had better 'phone the lawyer's wife again," suggested Ralph after a moment of thought. "Those fellows lurking around here might do the lawyer some harm."

Ralph went to the telephone. As he took down the receiver and applied it to his ear his expert knowledge of telegraphy gave him a quick intuition.

"Hello," he said, "we're off the circuit. Worse than that--the instrument is dead."

"Is that so?" said the tramp. "Then it explains what that sneaking fellow was doing on the roof. They've cut the telephone wires."

CHAPTER XXIII—ONE MINUTE AFTER TWELVE

The young railroader of Stanley Junction realized that he had assumed no ordinary risk or responsibility in acting the role of a trusted messenger in behalf of the old telegrapher in the train dispatcher's office at headquarters.

The situation at Derby had become an exciting and a critical one. Here was Ralph, the factory foreman and this tramp acquaintance cut off from the town, isolated in a lonely spot and surrounded by desperate and dangerous men who were bent on a mission of wreck and ruin.

Bartlett looked a little blank. The tramp grinned as was his wont. He looked as if he would not be sorry to engage in the "ruction" he had talked about, to get even with his treacherous enemies.

Ralph had grown a trifle uneasy. If the lawyer did not put in an appearance, it was difficult to foresee how affairs would turn out. He did not rely much on Bartlett's Winchester or the brawny fists of the tramp. The young train dispatcher had seen some pretty sharp and definite work done in the name of the law during a railroad strike, and from what he had heard of Dorsett he did not believe he would make a raid on the plant until he was very certain of successfully carrying out his wicked plans.

Ralph paced the floor of the little office lost in deep thought. The foreman watched him grimly from the corner of one eye. The tramp, lounging amid the unusual luxury of a big swivel chair, seemed enjoying hugely the comfort of the well-heated room and ready for anything that came along, now that he was no longer cold or hungry. He, too, watched Ralph, and as the latter with a kind of start: stopped in his walk and his face lightened up, the tramp drawled out:

"Something struck you, guv'nor--give it a voice."

"You're pretty sharp," said Ralph, with a smile at the speaker. Then he walked over to the foreman. "Mr. Bartlett," he continued, "I'd like to take a look through your plant here, if you've no objection."

"None at all, only I wonder why?" submitted Bartlett, with a searching glance at Ralph.

"I was thinking of something," explained Ralph--"how to beat those fellows who are coming here at midnight."

"I hope you've hit it!" exclaimed the foreman eagerly.

"We shall see."

Bartlett took a lantern, and leaving the tramp in the office he led Ralph into the large room adjoining. It was filled with long flat vats filled with some dark liquid. There was a sulphurous smell to the place. The foreman made no explanations until he reached the furnace room.

"You see those big tanks?" he spoke now. "Those are the melters. Mr. Glidden spent a great deal of money to get them right. Run up that ladder at the side and look over the rim."

Ralph did so. The tank he looked into was filled with bars that looked like lead, with smaller fragments of a darker metal and great chunks that resembled resin. When he came down to the floor he opened the door of the furnace underneath and peered in. His face took on a satisfied look.

"See here," said Bartlett, as they reëntered the big room on their way back to the office. "Those pipes running from each furnace convey the molten metal into those vats. There is a great hissing and bubbling, I can tell you. It's a sort of red-hot cyaniding process. The fumes, though! No man could walk through this room when the pour is on and come out alive."

"You don't say so?" murmured Ralph. Then he went up close to the foreman and took him by lapel of his coat.

"Mr. Bartlett," he said, "I see you are all ready to fire up."

"At a minute's notice," replied the foreman, with a gleam of pride in his eye.

"I suppose within an hour, two hours, you could get those melters so hot they are red all through?"

"Pretty nigh, I tell you."

"And you could fill this room here with fumes that would make a man hesitate about crossing the dead line, until you got ready to shut off the feeders?"

"You couldn't hit it closer if you'd been brought up to the business," declared the foreman with unction.

"Good. Now then--whisper."

They were near the office door. Ralph talked rapidly in a low tone into the ear of his companion. The latter gave a great start. Then he grinned. Then, alive with animation, he clapped Ralph mightily on the back.

"Lad," he cried with enthusiasm, "you're better than the lawyer and the whole constable force of Derby put together."

"What do you say about my plan?" inquired Ralph.

"Say--bully for you, that's what I say!" almost shouted the factory foreman.

"If you start at eleven o'clock you'll be ready when that gang arrives?"

"Ready, and time to spare. Say, but you've been thinking to some purpose."

The foreman burst into a gay whistle as he reëntered the office. The tramp regarded him searchingly, and then looked at Ralph as if he half guessed that they were up to something. He was too indolent, however, to delve for the facts.

The lawyer did not put in an appearance, Ralph knew by the whistles just what trains were arriving at Derby. The 8 p. m. came and passed on its way. Then the 10:30. By five minutes of eleven Ralph decided that the lawyer must have missed connection in some way, for he did not arrive at the plant.

Just as the office clock struck eleven, Ralph arose from his chair and walked up in front of the tramp.

"Do you want to earn a few dollars?" he inquired.

"Sure, that's me," answered the man--"what doing?"

"Helping Mr. Bartlett here. It will be hot work, but he'll do most of it, he tells me."

"Oh, in the factory here."

"Yes."

"I'd rather stay here in the office and handle that Winchester when the mob comes," observed the tramp.

"You can do ten times as much good doing what I want you to do."

"Will it have anything to do with knocking out Dorsett's plans?"

"Everything."

The tramp arose to his feet like a jumping jack, his face wearing an eager grin.

"Guv'nor," he said, "I'd trust you in most anything. I'd like to have a front seat out here to see the fun when the show begins, but if my being behind the scenes helps, depend on me."

"I do," said Ralph. "You go with Mr. Bartlett."

Ralph sat down as the two men disappeared. He listened attentively to the sounds from the melting room. Soon the big blast chimney began to roar, and glancing out of the window Ralph could see fitful red gleams shoot out upon the snow.

There was a speaking tube running from the office to Bartlett's post of duty. Soon it whistled, and the foreman announced:

"All ready."

"So am I," mused Ralph, as he counted the minutes roll away. He tried to imagine just what was going to happen and how he would meet the crisis when it arrived.

Midnight came, and one minute after twelve. Five, ten, fifteen minutes passed away. Then Ralph bent his ear. Some kind of a conveyance was coming down the turnpike. He could hear the ring of a horse's hoofs and the hard wheels crunching the frozen snow.

Ralph picked up a newspaper and pretended to read it, looking as comfortable and unconcerned as possible.

"Whoa!" sounded a loud voice outside.

Then other voices mingled in confusion. Some one came to the window and peered in. There was a muffled consultation outside. Finally a thunderous knock sounded at the door, and a stentorian voice shouted out:

"Open--in the name of the law!"

CHAPTER XXIV—THE BATTLE OF WITS

Ralph instantly arose to his feet and unlocked the office door. He was about to open it when it was forcibly burst inwards in his grasp.

"We want to get in here," vociferated a strident voice, and a consequential-looking little fellow, wearing his coat open so that a constable's badge showed on his vest, swept over the threshold as if he was leading an army to an attack.

"Certainly," said Ralph, with great politeness. "Come in, gentlemen--there's a good fire and enough chairs, I guess."

He was interested in quickly casting his eye over the marauding group. Six men had followed the constable in hot haste. One of them, who kept close to the officer, seemed to be his assistant. Four men, rough looking and with fiery breaths and faces, Ralph recognized as the group he had seen in the town that afternoon, two of whom had followed him to the lawyer's house.

The real leader of the party, however, was a man whom Ralph had never seen before. He at once surmised that this was Dorsett. The latter pushed the others aside and stepped up to Ralph insolently.

"Who are you?" he demanded, with a scowl of suspicion and dislike.

"I represent the brother of Mr. Glidden."

"Oh, you do?" sneered Dorsett. "I thought you was the office boy."

"Representative, hey?" snapped out the constable quickly. "Stand aside, Mr. Dorsett. This is the very person I wish to see."

The official made a great ado getting a bundle of papers out of his pocket. He selected one, flopped it open and fixed an imperious eye on Ralph.

"As agent de facto, ex officio, essettery, I present a demand against Henry William Glidden in the penal sum of four thousand one hundred and twenty-seven dollars and ninety-eight cents. Are you authorized to pay the same, deprosedendum, or forever hold your peace."

"I have one thousand dollars at the home of the lawyer," explained Ralph.

"Cash?" demanded the constable, licking his chops and blinking his eyes like a ravenous wolf at the mention of money.

"Yes, sir, and the balance will be here in Derby before court sits in the morning."

"Court don't sit any more in this case," growled out Dorsett, who all along had regarded Ralph with a leery eye. "Here's the court."

"I say, Dorsett, the lad talks business. One thousand dollars ain't to be sneezed at. So much on account, see? Just an appetizer. We'll gobble the whole outfit finally. Um-m-m--” and his voice died away into a drone into the ear of Dorsett only, who shook his head with the forcible words:

“No. I won’t lose a minute. Get at your job instantly.”

“Ha-hum,” observed the constable, flapping the document in his hand importantly and again approaching Ralph. “Ipse dixit de profundis--you refuse to pay this just claim?”

“It will be paid within the legal limit of time,” answered Ralph.

“The legal limit of time has elapsed,” declared the constable, “as witness this document.”

“Then I suppose you take possession?” said Ralph. “That is all right. As soon as Mr. Glidden’s brother arrives he will put up the cash or a bond and redeem the plant.”

“That can’t be done,” observed the constable. “Practically we are already in possession. The plaintiff, however, has sued out a writ extraordinary. As assignee of the original seller of the melting tanks, which were purchased, not on open account but on contract, and the same held delinquent, he has here in this document a writ of replevin. We want those tanks. The balance will come later.”

“Very well, gentlemen,” said Ralph coolly, “if you are sure you are within your legal rights, go ahead.”

The constable’s assistant made a rush for the iron door.

“Only,” continued Ralph impressively, “don’t try it through that room.”

“Hey--why not?” demanded the constable, pricking up his ears.

“Because the corroding vats are in action, and one minute in that poisonous air would smother the last one of you.”

“Hah!” ejaculated the constable, “we shall see.”

He advanced to the iron door and lifted its hasped bar.

“Whew!” he gurgled, slamming it shut again, one whiff sending him reeling back as though he had been hit with a club.

“Tricked us, have you,” gritted Dorsett, darting a malevolent look at Ralph. “Get around to the rear, you four. Smash out those barred windows.”

“I submit,” interposed Ralph calmly, “that won’t do any good. The tanks are red hot and will remain so for many hours.”

“Baffled!” hissed the constable dramatically. “Dorsett, they’ve got the drop on you. No, no,” continued the official, lifting his hand as the infuriated

Dorsett seemed about to dash out of the office bent on any destruction, so long as he carried out his evil designs, "law is law."

"And you've got a writ to execute it, haven't you?" yelled Dorsett.

"Not with violence, my dear sir--not with violence," mildly intimated the constable. "I fear we have proceeded with undue haste. I assumed that the plant would be inactive."

"It was, up to last evening."

"On that hypothesis we took out a writ for immediate seizure of certain specified chattels. You may enter, seize, and distrain. You may stretch a point and force a door or smash a window, but you have no warrant to batter down a wall. If you did--red hot, see?" and with a rather sickly smile the speaker went through a pantomime of seizing and briskly dropping an overheated object.

"Then take possession," commanded Dorsett stormily. "Get this young marplot out of here and let no more of his ilk in again."

"Sorry," retorted the constable, "but there again we have checkmated ourselves. Relying to your statements we took extreme measures to tear out the tanks and later put a custodian in charge. We cannot now legally enter here or remain here except on a new writ of possession."

Now was Ralph's hour of triumph and he could not refrain from smiling to himself. Dorsett noticed it and thrashed about like a madman. He did not assault the quiet unpretentious lad who held him and his scowling myrmidons at bay, but he looked as if he would like to have done so.

Finally Dorsett quieted down. He drew the constable to one side of the room and they held a rapid consultation. Then the constable's assistant was beckoned to join them, and later two of Dorsett's allies.

This trio left the office instructed by the constable to hasten to the magistrate in the next township who had issued the replevin writ, and secure a broader document for possession of the premises.

Calm fell over the place at their departure. Meantime the furnaces at the rear of the plant roared on merrily, and Ralph mentally calculated how long it would be before they cooled down and Dorsett got his itching fingers in play to cripple and destroy.

Perhaps an hour went by. The marauding party was lounging and dozing. Ralph bent his ear to listen as a locomotive whistle in the distance told of the passage of a train from the north.

The young dispatcher knew the schedule like a book. No train was due till daybreak. A second outburst of tooting signals informed and electrified him.

"A special!" he murmured, fired up magically. "Can it be possible--"

Ralph paused there, checking the wild thoughts, or rather hopes, that thronged his mind. He was thinking of the belated lawyer as well as of the old telegraph operator.

The office clock gave out three sharp strokes as there was a commotion. Some one tried the door. It was not locked and opened at the touch. Ralph jumped to his feet with an irrepressible cry of gladness.

Two men entered. One was the old headquarters dispatcher, Glidden. His companion, a peaked faced, shrewd eyed man, Ralph intuitively accepted as the Derby lawyer.

"Hello!" shot out the latter spicily--"visitors, friends. How's this, Dorsett?"

"We've come to stay, that's how it is," growled out the man addressed.

"I think not," spoke up Ralph quickly. "They have stolen a march on you, Mr. Glidden. They came with a replevin writ, found it of no effect, and have now sent to some renegade justice outside of the township for a writ of possession."

"Have, eh?" said the lawyer. "Well, I fancy they won't use it. Here, you, constable--what's your authority?"

"Demand--four thousand one seventy-seven ninety-eight," pronounced the official, waving a document.

"How is it, Mr. Glidden?" inquired the lawyer.

The old dispatcher rammed his hand in his shirt and drew out a formidable roll of bank notes.

"I've got thirty five hundred here," he said. "Fairbanks has a thousand."

"I left it in the safe up at your house," explained Ralph to the lawyer.

"All right, I guess my check is good for that balance, eh, constable?"

"Yes, surely," answered the officer obsequiously, thinking of further legal business.

"Cancel the judgment," ordered the lawyer. "Now, then, Dorsett, I reckon we can dispense with your company."

The baffled conspirators sneaked away with dark mutterings. The lawyer hailed through the speaking tube.

"I got so anxious I arranged for a special at Hillsdale," explained Glidden to Ralph. "Just by luck I ran across the lawyer, waiting for a train."

It was after Bartlett and the tramp had shut down the furnaces and appeared in the office room and the foreman explained Ralph's clever plans of the night, that the lawyer approached the young train dispatcher and placed a friendly hand on his shoulder.

"Young man," he said, "did you ever study law?"

"No, sir. Somewhere along the line I would like to, but just now railroading takes up my time."

"H'm. Very good. Well, if you ever want to, I'll give you a job."

"Thank you, sir."

"Yes," added the lawyer, with a bright admiring glance at Ralph's face, "in fact, after your clever work to-night, I think I would be willing to take you into partnership."

CHAPTER XXV—A WILD NIGHT

"Tic-tac!"--"annul train 22--blockade at Fox Center"--"25-25-25-45 stalled at Morey Gap." "Fast freight derailed--switch 19 outside of Abingdon."

"Whew!" exploded the first trick man at dispatcher's headquarters. "Did you get all that, Fairbanks?"

Ralph nodded, but did not speak. He was too busy for that. His hand was constantly on the key of his instrument, and his ear was bent with almost painful tension to catch every faint vibration of the wires. His eyes jumped with magic swiftness from chart to note sheet and train schedule. Ralph just now was a typical dispatcher in the midst of muddles, calls, cross-calls and piling up business enough to distract the average man. The young railroader confessed to himself that this was the busiest hour of his life.

It was a wild, stormy night outside, cozy enough in the warm, well-lighted dispatcher's room. The wind without went howling by shrilly. Great sweeps of snow deluged the window panes. Whistles from the yards sounded hoarse and muffled. Inside that room skilled intelligence and vigilance controlled the midnight workings of the important Great Northern. In a picture view Ralph could see some belated locomotive breasting the drifts of lonely gully and curve. He could imagine a cumbersome freight feeling its way slowly past snow-clouded signals, marooned station men with their instruments knocked dead through fallen wires, and the venturesome repair crew wading through deep drifts to locate the break.

And a finger on the key controlled all this mix-up, and intent eye and brain tried to keep the various trains moving. As early as eight o'clock messages had begun to come in fast and thick telling of the great storm of wind and snow, the third of the season, that was sweeping over the Mountain Division of the Great Northern road.

At ten o'clock the commercial wires went out from Rockton, and a special operator now sat over in a corner of the dispatcher's room at an extra instrument taking press news over a roundabout circuit. Everything went by jerks and starts. The insulation was bad and sometimes the sounders moved without giving out any intelligible vibration.

Towards eleven o'clock the rush was over on regular business, but the delayed train list began to pile up alarmingly. Everything was late. Within the next half hour two blockades, four stalled freights and two telegraph lines down were reported. It was now that Ralph was put distinctly on his mettle. Glidden watched him anxiously but admiringly from under his deep set eyebrows, and so far did not have to check up an error in orders or a mistake in judgment.

On either side of Ralph was a card. That on the right hand side had the names of all the stations from Stanley Junction to Rockton. The one on the left side had all the stations from Rockton to Stanley Junction. On both cards some of the stations had been crossed off, particularly on the right hand card. In fact only one station this side of terminus remained.

Glidden went quickly over to Ralph's table as a message ticked out that both had been waiting for. With a somewhat triumphant smile Ralph checked off the last station with a dash of his pencil.

"Gone through, eh?" spoke Glidden with a grin.

"Safe and snug," answered Ralph. "You heard--one hour late on account of the snow, but no attack."

"Good thing for the conspirators," observed Glidden. "Either they found out it was a trap or saw the half dozen armed guards inside."

"Perhaps they fancied we knew too much and gave up the experiment of robbing the pay car."

"Well, she's through--now for the other one. How is it?"

"Heavy snow, but she's making time," reported Ralph, glancing at the remaining card. "83 is a hundred miles out of Rockton. Just passed Shoreham on the Mountain Division."

"Say, those fellows will never guess what they've missed till it's too late, hey?"

"It seems so," nodded Ralph.

There was a lapse of messages now. Only the ceaseless grind of press dispatches clicked from the instrument over in the corner. Ralph sat back and took a breathing spell.

The pay car had gone through--the dummy pay car rather--which had left the Junction at eight o'clock that morning. It had been loaded up pretentiously with the apparent usual bags of coin and little safes that were used on regular trips. These, however, contained no money. The paymaster went aboard ostentatiously. The doors and windows were securely locked as usual. Inside, however, were half a dozen men armed to the teeth. The dummy pay car was a bait for the robbers. They had not appeared. The cypher message to Ralph just received told him that the train had reached terminus without hindrance or damage.

"Now for the other one," Glidden had said. This meant a good deal. The "other one" was the real pay car, loaded with real treasure. To checkmate any possible attack, the railroad officials with great secrecy had loaded up an ordinary baggage car with the pay safes and bullion in transit for banks.

It was proposed to distribute this in parcels at section centers out of the usual routine.

So far it looked as if it would be smooth sailing except for the snow storm. No. 83 was reported as having passed over one hundred miles on the route. There was a train hand on guard on the front platform of the car and two guards inside, according to the advices Ralph had received.

The impromptu pay car had been hitched to the rear of a long train of milk cars. This had been done because she was to be switched at four different points before she reached Stanley Junction. The pay safes had been boxed up and burlapped, giving the appearance of ordinary freight.

There was some inconsequential messages during the ensuing half hour. Then a chance to tally on the route card on Ralph's table as No. 83 was reported to have passed Fletcher, one hundred and twenty-five miles out of Rockton.

Then the commercial wire slowed down for a spell. The operator got up, stretching his cramped fingers.

"Snow two feet on the level at Rockton," he reported, "and coming down like an avalanche. Why don't they send me 30? I've got the grist up to 29. Hello, here she comes. No, she don't. Another item."

The operator jumped to his instrument and began to flimsy the message. Ralph arose sharply from his chair. He had lost most of the message, but one part of it had caught his hearing.

It startled him, for a name had tapped out clear and distinct, a familiar name--Glen Palmer.

CHAPTER XXVI—AN AMAZING ANNOUNCEMENT

The press operator rapidly wrote out the message coming over the wire, took the finished sheet, folded it, and sent it down a chute. This led to the room below where messengers were waiting for the service. The duplicate sheet he slipped over a spindle. Ralph hurriedly reached his side.

"Let me look at that last flimsy, will you?"

"Cert," bobbed the accommodating operator, handing it to Ralph.

The latter read the hurriedly traced lines with a falling face.

"That's my 30," announced the operator, shutting off his key and arising to drop work for the night.

Ralph paid no attention to him. The young railroader was conscious of a decidedly painful impression. He had heard nothing of Glen Palmer or his grandfather since the night the jumbled up "Look out for the pay car" telegram had arrived. Ralph, however, had frequently thought of the lad whom he had started in at the chicken farm.

Young Palmer had been disappointing. All along the line Ralph had to admit this. Once in a while, however, when he realized the lonely bedouin-like existence of Glen, certain pity and indulgence were evoked. Now, however, a grave, hurt look came into Ralph's eyes.

"Too bad," he said, softly and sorrowfully. "I fancy Bob Adair was right."

The road detective had forcibly expressed the opinion that Glen Palmer had been a jail bird. More than that, Adair believed him to be in league with the conspirators. Ralph thought not. Glen had sent him two warning messages under extraordinary circumstances. The press telegram just over the wires, however, certainly coincided with the charges of Ike Slump that Glen was a criminal.

It was one of a batch of items that had come over the commercial line that evening. The message was dated at a small interior city, Fordham, and it read:

"The system adopted by the Bon Ton department store here to discourage theft, bore practical results today, and their publicly offered reward of ten dollars was claimed by an amateur detective. The latter discovered a boy in the act of removing a valuable ring from a display tray, and informed on him. The thief was searched and the stolen article found secreted on his person. He unblushingly admitted his guilt. The thief gave the name of Sam Jones, but some papers found on him disclosed his correct name, which is Glen Palmer. He was brought before Justice Davis, who sentenced him promptly to sixty days in the county workhouse."

"What's hitting you so glum, Fairbanks?" inquired Glidden, as Ralph kept poring over the telegram in a depressed way.

"A friend of mine gone wrong," replied Ralph simply.

He was glad that he was not called on for any further explanation. Just then Tipton broke in with a crisp short wire--No. 83 had just passed, only fifteen minutes late.

"She's getting in among the bad mountain cuts," observed Glidden, as Ralph crossed off the station on his check card. "If the pull isn't too hard, I reckon she'll make her first switch nearly on time."

There was now in the dispatcher's room a dead calm of some duration. Glidden sat figuring up some details from the business of the night. Ralph rested back in his chair, thinking seriously of Glen Palmer, and wondering what mystery surrounded him and his grandfather.

The silence was broken finally with a sharp tanging challenge, always stimulating and startling to the operator. It was the manager's call:

"25--25--25."

Ralph swept his key in prompt response.

"Hello!" said the aroused Glidden, listening keenly, "thought Tipton was off for the night after 83 had passed. What's--that!"

Ralph, deeply intent, took in the rapid tickings eagerly. The message was from the station which had reported No. 83 passed in good shape three-quarters of an hour before.

Here was the hurry message that came over the wire:

"83 something wrong. Just found brakeman of train lying in snow at side of track. Hurt or drugged. Mumbled about foul play. Catch Maddox and advise conductor of 83."

"I say!" exclaimed Glidden, jumping to his feet. "Get Maddox, Fairbanks. 83 is due or passed."

"M-x M-x--stop 83," tapped Ralph quickly.

"Too late," muttered Glidden in a sort of groan. "Thunder! she can't be reached till she gets to Fairview, forty miles ahead."

Maddox had wired back to headquarters the following message:

"83 just passed after coaling. Fairview reports four feet of snow in the cuts. No stop this side."

Then Ralph did the only thing he could. He wired to the operator at Fairview:

"Hold 83 on arrival for special orders."

The sleepy look left Glidden's eyes and Ralph was all nerved up. There had come a break in the progress of the substitute pay car, and both felt anxiously serious as to its significance.

"There's something mighty wrong in this business," declared Glidden.

"It looks that way," assented Ralph.

"Get Tipton."

Ralph called over the wire and repeated.

"Something has shut out Tipton," he reported.

"Wires down or cut," observed Glidden. "Try Maddox."

Ralph did so.

"Maddox not open," he said. His mind ran over the situation. He recalled a night like this when he and Fireman Fogg had run alone a battered locomotive over the same stretch of road on a Special for President Grant of the Great Northern. It had been a hairbreadth experience, and he wondered if No. 83 would get through.

One o'clock--two o'clock. The young dispatcher and his first trick man found it hard to endure the irksome monotony of those two anxious hours. It was like a tensioned cord breaking when at last the welcome call from Fairview came over the wires.

"83," the message ticked out, "crippled; six feet of snow ahead, and will have to lay over. Send orders."

"She's got through safe, that's a consolation," said Glidden, with a vast sigh of satisfaction.

Ralph simply clicked an "O. K." It had been arranged that at Fairview the conductor would wire for instructions. These had been purposely withheld for secrecy's sake. A transfer of two pay safes was due at the next station and Ralph waited, knowing that as soon as he could leave his train the conductor would send a personal message.

Suddenly the instrument began to click again.

"From conductor 83: metaphor, resolve, adirondacks, typists."

"What!" shouted Glidden, jumping to his feet in a frenzy.

Ralph's hand shook and the color left his face.

Translated, the message from the conductor of train No. 83 meant:

"The substitute pay car has disappeared."

CHAPTER XXVII—THE STOLEN PAY CAR

Long before the whistles blew for seven o'clock at Stanley Junction the news had spread like wildfire--train No. 83, carrying the substitute pay car, containing two hundred thousand dollars in cash and a king's ransom in bullion for the banks, had disappeared.

Somewhere between Fairview and Maddox, the time, and means unknown, the car containing all this treasure had been boldly stolen, disconnected from the train, had vanished.

One minute after receiving the startling cypher message, Ralph had telephoned to the superintendent of the road at his home in Stanley Junction. Within an hour that official and two assistants in hastily donned garb and with perturbed faces were at headquarters trying to solve a situation enshrouded in the densest mystery.

The wires were kept hot with messages to and from Fairview. The conductor of No. 83 could simply repeat his amazing story. When the train arrived at Maddox they found the precious treasure car missing. Their crippled engine could not be brought into service. The snow-clogged rails offered no chance for a hand car.

Had the car broken loose? was the question put. No, was the answer. The bumper of the last milk car showed no evidences of unusual strain or break. The coupling pin had simply been removed, how far back the line it was impossible to surmise, certainly between Fairview and Maddox.

And then, linking in the discovery of the brakeman lying drugged or hurt at the side of the track by the station agent at Tipton, the irresistible conclusion was arrived at by the anxious railroad officials that their careful plans to delude the conspirators and safely get the substitute pay car through had failed utterly.

There was only one thing to do. This was to make an immediate search for the missing car. Belleville, ten miles distant from Fairview, was wired an urgency call. The snowplow service with one caboose was ordered out. The division superintendent at Belleville was instructed concerning the situation, and at four a. m. the train started for Fairview, to plow its way back over the route of No. 83 to seek a trace of the missing car.

It was before daylight when a report came in. Nowhere along the sharp curves or deep gullies of the route was a single trace of the car discovered. It had disappeared as absolutely and completely as if the earth had opened and swallowed it up.

The falling snow had obliterated all recent marks on its surface. By the merest chance, ten miles out of Maddox, the division superintendent had noticed a small mound that was unfamiliar. Stopping the train, an investigation disclosed the two guards who had been locked in the pay car when it left Rockton.

It had been hard work to arouse the men, but finally one of them was restored to consciousness sufficiently to relate a clear story.

Their instructions had been simple--to use their rifles if any stranger attempted to enter the car on its journey. Between stations the brakeman on duty on the rear platform of the car was allowed to enter to get warm. He had always, however, given an agreed-on signal at the door of the car.

It was just after leaving Tipton that his familiar knock had called one of them to the door to let him in. Taken completely off their guard, as four men one after the other jumped in among them, the guards had no opportunity to seize their firearms. They had been knocked down on the floor of the car, cloths drugged with some subtle acid had been held over their faces. They knew no more until they had been discovered by the division superintendent.

"It's easy to guess it out," whispered Glidden to Ralph while the officials in the room were piecing all these bits of information together.

"Yes," responded Ralph, "the conspirators in some way received advance information of every step we intended to make."

"They must have got aboard secretly beyond Tipton, or have been hidden in the last milk car," suggested Glidden. "They jumped on and doped the brakeman, disposed of him, later of the two guards, and were in possession. The division superintendent reports that the wires were found cut just out of Tipton. The crowd had planned out everything to a second, with conspirators posted all along the line."

"But the missing car," said Ralph thoughtfully; "what has become of it?"

Neither he nor Glidden could figure out a solution of this difficult problem. Even the experienced official after a long confab gave it up. The only thing they could do was to order a hasty search for Bob Adair, the road detective, to rush to the spot with all the force he needed.

The superintendent spoke pleasantly to Ralph and Glidden as the day force relieved them. He even forgot his anxieties long enough to commend them for the hard work they had done and the close tab they had kept on all the occurrences of the night.

"It's a bad mess for the Great Northern," he said with a worried face, "and it proves that our enemies are not as dull as we thought they were."

Ralph went home tired out. He found it hard, however, to get to sleep. The strain and excitement of the preceding twelve hours told severely on his nerves. All through the morning his vivid dreams were of snow blockades, cut wires, and stolen treasure cars.

On account of their special service on behalf of the pay car affair, Glidden and himself were relieved from duty for twenty-four hours. The old dispatcher dropped in at the Fairbanks home shortly after noon.

"Have they found any trace of the missing pay car?" at once inquired Ralph.

"Stolen, you mean," corrected Glidden. "No. Theories? Lots of them. She was simply cut off from the train. She couldn't have derailed, for there's no trace of that unless she went up in the air. Of course, whoever manipulated her sent her off on a siding among the mountains on a down grade."

"And that is the last known of it. Well, what later?"

"Adair will be over to find out soon, or else he won't," retorted Glidden crisply. "You know that web of old abandoned sidings and spurs branching out the other side of Maddox?"

"Near Eagle Pass, you mean?"

"Yes. The superintendent thinks the car will be found somewhere on the branches, looted, of course, for the robbers have had hours to handle the booty."

Nothing but theory, however, resulted from official investigations during the ensuing two days. The following Monday morning the assistant superintendent met Ralph on his way to work. The missing car problem was still unsolved, he told the young railroader.

Adair and his men had explored every spur and siding the entire length of Eagle Pass. Not a trace of the stolen car had been discovered, and the road officer was working on a theory that it might have been run off on connecting private switches onto the Midland Central, and the collusion of important influences exercised.

When Ralph got home that evening he found an old time friend awaiting him. It was Zeph Dallas, just arrived.

"Why, hello!" hailed Ralph heartily, walking into the sitting room where he had spied Zeph. "I'm glad to see you, Zeph--why, what's the matter?"

Zeph was indeed an object to excite wonderment and attention. His face was about the forlornest that Ralph had ever seen. His eyes were like two holes burned in his head, his clothes were wrinkled as if he had slept in them for a week.

In a limp, hopeless fashion the "boy detective," all his plumes of ambition sadly trailing in the dust of humiliation and defeat, allowed his hand to rest lifelessly in that of Ralph. His throat choked up with a sob, and his eyes filled with tears.

"Ralph," he almost whispered, "they've fooled me, I'm beaten out."

"You mean the men who stole the pay car?"

"Yes; oh, they put it over on me good. They pulled the wool over my eyes. I thought I had them, and they let me think so. I've got to find them, I've got to make good, or I'll never hold up my head in Stanley Junction again."

"You did the best you could, I am sure, Zeph," encouraged Ralph soothingly.

"The best won't do!" almost shouted out Zeph. "There's got to be better. Oh, Ralph, it will break my heart if I fail. I've got to find that stolen pay car, and you've got to help me."

CHAPTER XXVIII—THE "TEST" SPECIAL

"Mr. Fairbanks?"

"Yes, sir."

"This is the office of the general superintendent. He wishes to see you immediately."

"I will report at once."

Ralph put down the telephone receiver, exchanged his office coat for street wear, and within five minutes was admitted into the private office of his superior official.

The superintendent looked bothered and his eyes were fixed on a great array of documents on the desk before him. Ralph's brisk step and bright face seemed to rouse him, and with a word of welcome he said:

"Sit down, Fairbanks." Ralph wondered why he had been sent for. He hoped it was concerning the pay car mystery. There was not an hour in the day that in some shape or other this perplexing puzzle did not come up before him. More than one of his friends was vitally interested in the outcome of that baffling case. For the sake of Bob Adair and Zeph Dallas, he sincerely wished that the mists of secrecy and vagueness might be cleared away.

"Unfinished business," spoke the superintendent after a pause, almost irritably brushing aside a heap of papers directly before him. "Will it ever be finished?" he added with a sigh. "Fairbanks," and the official singled out a letter from among the heap of documents, "I am afraid I must ask you to go on special duty."

"Very well, sir," said Ralph at once.

"Always ready, always willing," commended the superintendent with an approving glance at the young railroader. "I wish there were more like you, Fairbanks. You know the bother and stress we are in. This pay car business has upset the whole official force, and we are still in the dark."

"But Mr. Adair is on the case," submitted Ralph.

"It has been of no use. He has made an investigation along every inch of the road where the car might have disappeared. He has given up, discouraged. Here is his last report. He mentions you."

"Mentions me?" repeated Ralph.

"Yes. That is one reason why I have sent for you. He reports from Fairview, and asks us to send you to him on Wednesday."

"That is day after tomorrow," said Ralph.

"Exactly. What his plans are I cannot tell you, but he refers to some efficient work you have done in his line in the past, and requests us to detail you specially in his service. What do you say, Fairbanks?"

"I am at your orders, sir."

"Very good. That settles one part of the business. The other may not come so welcome to you, but you must be our man. Glance over that, will you?"

The official handed Ralph a card covered with calculations. There were bewildering figures, so many cars, so many used per day, so much profit. The totals were enormous.

"The Overland Fruit Dispatch," explained the superintendent, "is out for bids on the transfer of their cars east from Rockton."

"I heard something of that."

"We are out for the contract. It means a big thing for us. So is the Midland Central. That means war, or, rather, more war. Their schedule beats ours by ten minutes. We must beat them by two hours. The test run began at ten o'clock this morning. Porter and Winston, both good men, run as far as Portland. I am not afraid in broad daylight. Nearly all the trouble has been east of that point--you understand?"

"Perfectly," assented Ralph--"you are afraid of some trickery on the part of our rivals?"

"Yes. I want you to reach Portland and catch the special at four p. m. If the new locomotive crew look good to you, just superintend. But rush that train into the yards by the stroke of eleven p. m., or we lose the contract."

"I think I can do it," said Ralph.

"Very well, we give you free rein. Dismiss the crew and find a new one, as you like. You have orders for clear tracks over everything else. Lay out your schedule, give Glidden charge of the wires at headquarters, and get us that contract."

"I will catch the first west through and report at eleven o'clock to-night," promised Ralph confidently.

"Good for you, Fairbanks," commended the superintendent, slapping Ralph encouragingly on the shoulder.

The next was a busy hour for Ralph. He studied the schedules, posted Glidden, took a hurry run for home and caught the train just as it was pulling out of the depot. Ralph reached Portland at half-past three in the afternoon.

The special was on time and due in thirty minutes. She was to take water and coal at the yards, and Ralph, making himself known to the operator there, loitered outside. He saw the relief engineer appear. He was a man he did not know, and something about his face and manner impressed the young railroader rather unfavorably.

The man set his dinner pail near the steps of the switch tower and walked about with the air of a person looking for some one. Then at a low whistle he started for a pile of ties some distance away. A man lurking there had beckoned to him. Ralph watched closely but drew back out of view. His keenest wits were on the alert in a second. He had recognized the lurker as a former unreliable employe of the Great Northern, discharged at the time of the great strike.

Ralph feared this fellow might recognize him and dared not approach him any nearer. The twain conversed for only a moment. Then the lurker handed the engineer a bag. It held apparently about a bushel of some kind of stuff. The engineer took it and returned to the tower, his companion disappearing.

Just then the special came down the tracks. The locomotive was disconnected and the tired and grimed crew drove for the dog house.

In a minute or two the relief engine came down the tracks in charge of the fireman of the run. Ralph looked over the man. He had all the appearances of an honest, plodding fellow. After he had hitched to the train he got down to oil some cylinders. The engineer piled aboard with his bag, chucked it under the seat, and alighted again and went back to meet the conductor from the caboose.

Of that bag Ralph had been suspicious from the start. He now deftly took the engine step, hauled out the bag, thrust it under the fireman's seat, swung shut its swinging board, and sat down at the engineer's post.

"Hello!" exclaimed the fireman, stepping up into the cab--"who are you?"

"Your engineer this trip."

"Eh? Where does Bartley come in?"

"He don't come in," replied Ralph definitely.

"Your name Bartley?" inquired Ralph, as the engineer and the conductor came up to the locomotive.

"That's me," smartly responded the man with a wondering look at Ralph.

"Well, you are relieved from duty on this special trip," advised Ralph.

"Hey--who says so?"

"The general superintendent. Is that right, operator?"

The towerman nodded, beckoned Bartley aside and made some explanations to him. His auditor looked sullen and ugly. Ralph did not leave the post of duty he had assumed, meantime giving the conductor an idea of how affairs stood.

"Hold on, there," spoke Bartley in a gruff tone, as the train got ready to start out. "I've got some personal property in that cab."

"All right," nodded Ralph in quite a friendly way--"get it out."

"Bag of apples for a mate down the line," mumbled the engineer, reaching under the seat. "Bag of--thunder! they've gone."

The conductor had run to the caboose. The engineer drew back from the empty void under the seat in a puzzled, baffled way. Ralph beckoned to the operator.

"Watch that man," he ordered in a quick whisper. "If he tries to send any messages ahead advise the operator to report instantly to headquarters."

Then Ralph opened the throttle and sent the test special on her dubious way, leaving the discomfited Bartley glaring after him in baffled suspicion and distrust.

CHAPTER XXIX—"CRACK THE WHIP!"

"What's up--something?" declared the fireman of the special as the train cleared the yards at Portland.

"Yes," replied Ralph, watching out for signals and testing gauges and airbrakes. "This is up: What kind of a man is your engineer, Bartley?"

"He's not my engineer at all," retorted the fireman rather testily, "and I was sorry when I was listed with him. He's a bossing, quarrelsome sort of a fellow. He don't train with my crowd, and I'm glad you're on in his place. You're Fairbanks, eh? Well, I've heard of you."

"Nothing bad, I hope," challenged Ralph with a smile.

"Almost too good to last."

"Oh, by the way, I want to say to you that this trip is going to give you a great chance."

"For what?" inquired the fireman, big eyed and interested.

"To make a record."

"It isn't much of a run."

"Yes, it is, and a great deal depends on it. The general superintendent is watching this run. It means a record and money for the Great Northern. We may strike trouble. Everything depends on landing these cars in the yards at Stanley Junction by eleven p. m. to-night."

"I'm with you, Mr. Fairbanks," said the fireman earnestly. "I don't know all you do, but I'll follow orders to a T."

"That's the ticket. Look here."

They were running easily over an air line, and Ralph had an opportunity to reach under the fireman's seat and pull into view the bag he had stored there.

"I say, who put that there?" demanded the fireman with a stare.

"I did. It belonged to Bartley. It's the 'personal property' he was so anxiously searching for."

Both looked into the bag. Ralph reached in and drew out a white object about the size of an egg. There were a good many others of these in the bag. It crisped in his fingers, as he turned it over inspecting it. He smelled of it, tasted of it, and a queer looking smile hovered over his lips.

"Do you know what it is?" he inquired.

The fireman fumbled it gingerly and then shook his head in the negative.

"It's soda--caustic soda," said Ralph. "There's enough more in there to start a laundry. This black stuff," and he drew out one of a hundred dark colored cubes--"it tastes like salt. Ah, I think I guess it out. Witness this," he continued to the fireman, "Bartley sneaked that bag aboard. I wish to keep it for evidence."

"Evidence of what?"

"Trickery, conspiracy. To my way of thinking he intended using that soda to churn the water in the boiler, and half a dozen of those salt bricks would smother the best fire you ever built."

"Thunder!" ejaculated the fireman excitedly, "there is something up, indeed."

"So much so, that we want to keep our eyes wide open every foot of the way," said Ralph emphatically. "In my opinion Bartley was bribed to cripple this locomotive so she couldn't pull through on time."

"The villain!" commented the fireman.

"Now all we've got to do is to beat that game," resumed Ralph, "and I'll guarantee you honorable mention and a raise if you help me."

"Anybody would help you," declared the fireman enthusiastically, gratified at the confidence reposed on him--"they don't raise such engineers as you every day."

"I am a dispatcher at present," said Ralph, "and a trifle rusty at the old trade, I find."

Rusty or not, Ralph now entered heartily into the zest of pushing the special through. Twenty miles on the main, to shorten the route a run was started over the Itica branch, forty miles in length. The special had full swing for the east, as headquarters was keeping tab of the train every minute.

There was a stop at Laketon, thirty miles farther on. It came on signal, and Ralph expected something had happened. He read twice the flimsy handed to him by the operator.

It was from the dispatcher at Portland, but via Glidden at headquarters. It advised Ralph that the treacherous engineer, Bartley, had sent a cypher dispatch to some one at Itica.

Itica was ten miles ahead. Here the Great Northern branch tracks crossed those of the rival road on the signal interlocking system.

"I will be glad when we get past Itica," decided Ralph mentally, after a sharp twenty minutes' run, as he came in sight of the crossing tower and got the stop signal; a glance ahead told him that it was doubtful if he got past Itica at all.

There was a single track at this point, and it crossed here the double track of the rival line. Blocking the Great Northern completely, a double-header stood slantwise, sagging where it had torn up the ground ripping out a cross-section of the interlocking rails.

The switchman came up to the special as Ralph slowed down.

"It's stalled, you are," he observed.

"I see that," said Ralph.

"A thrick."

"You think that, do you?"

"I know it. 'Twas done a-purpose. We've had no kind of throuble here before. They just pulled those two old wrecks to the crossing and derailed them a-purpose."

Ralph left his fireman in charge of the engine and ran up into the signal tower. He came down in a few minutes and consulted with the conductor. The fireman studied his set grave face intently as he resumed his place at the throttle. Ralph pulled the whistle as a back up signal. Then the train, composed of ten refrigerator fruit cars and the caboose, began retracing the course the special had just come.

Ten miles backing, and the special arrived at the station where Ralph had received the message from headquarters. He had a brisk brief talk with the operator there, calling the conductor into the consultation. There was some switching, and the locomotive, headed right, started from the main in a southerly direction.

"I say, Mr. Fairbanks," the fireman expressed himself in some wonderment, "of course you know where you are going."

"I hope I do."

"Well, I don't," blankly confessed the fireman. "This is the old Eagle Pass cut off, isn't it?"

"It was, once. I hope it is now."

"Why, it hasn't been used for years."

"We're going to use it."

The fireman looked blank. Except for some old fashioned targets, there was nothing to show that they were traversing the rails, for the snow lay on a dead level.

"I can't go back the main forty miles, make up forty more, and get to the Junction anywhere near schedule," explained Ralph. "We have already lost time from that blockade at Itica our rivals fixed up for us. If we can get through to the Mountain Division tracks over this stretch, We save over two hours' time."

"Aha, I see your idea," exclaimed the fireman, aroused. "I'm with you."

Ralph was trying a dangerous experiment, and he knew it. Time was the essential, however, and the risk must be taken. They felt their way cautiously. It was nearly dusk now, and he did not fancy getting caught after dark among those lonely mountain gullies.

The pilot had to clear the way of snow. There was a tremendous rattling of the coaches as they sunk with the track and struck uneven reaches. At a trestle structure the train shook visibly. The fireman uttered a great sigh of relief as the last car passed safely over it.

They were on a down slant on a sharp curve when a shock that was something terrific ran through the train. Ralph threw on the air lightning quick and closed the throttle with a jerk.

The young railroader was fairly lifted from his seat and the fireman went spinning to the bottom of the cab.

"Thunder!" he shouted, "what have we struck?"

Ralph got down to find out. The conductor came running up while he was making his inspection. They discovered a queer situation.

Chained to the track were three ties. They did not look as if they had been placed there for a bumper. But Ralph did not waste time theorizing. With what tools the locomotive afforded they set to work and soon removed the obstruction.

Just an hour later they cleared the old rickety cut off. It was dark now. They ran down the main line ten miles, and at The Barrens took coal and water, while Ralph was busy with the station operator in communication with headquarters.

He calculated closely as they started on the long home run. It would take some steam and the best of luck to reach the yards at Stanley Junction by eleven p. m.

At nine o'clock they passed Revere without stopping. At ten they switched at Wayne, forty-five miles from terminus.

It lacked just ten minutes of eleven o'clock when the special came in sight of the lights of the Junction. To follow the main and risk a stoppage at the limits would never allow of an arrival on the time set.

"I have got an idea," said Ralph, slowing up as they neared the first siding of the yards in-tracks.

"Go to it, then--anything to pull through on time," responded the fireman with vigor.

Ralph jumped down from the cab, unset a switch, glanced ahead down the open track, and then glanced at his watch.

"Eight minutes," he said, quite excited now. "Crowd on every pound of steam you can. We may make it by a bare scratch."

Ahead was the outline of the fence of the yards. The gate to its west special track outlet was shut after working hours, Ralph knew well, but it was a flimsy affair used less for protection than to exclude intruders.

"Four minutes," he spoke, and the flying locomotive was rushing ahead with a grinding roar.

"Three."

They took the gate, sending its frail boards flying up into the air in a cascade of riven splinters.

"Arrived!" shouted the fireman triumphantly.

Ralph started to let down speed. Just then something happened. The brake beam of the truck under the tender dropped, causing the wheels to leave the rails.

The locomotive played a veritable "crack the whip" with the cars behind, became separated from the train, and traveled fully four hundred feet before she stopped.

The train broke in three sections. The wheels seemed to be smashing through logs, rails and stones. The noise was deafening. A yardman said later that as the train burst through the switches each car seemed to carry beneath it a huge ball of fire, caused by the wheels being dead-locked by the automatic brakes.

Not a car was smashed, and no two cars were left on the same tracks or pointing the same way. The caboose had its rear wheels on one track and its front wheels on the track south. The cars were standing in every direction, but not a person was hurt, not a car was invalided.

Ralph ran up to the yardmaster and held out his watch to him.

"Verify the arrival," he ordered hastily.

"Yes, 10:58, two minutes ahead of time," said the man with a stare of wonderment. "We were expecting you, Fairbanks, but--not in that way!"

CHAPTER XXX—THE PAY CAR ROBBER

Ralph Fairbanks sat at work on the task apportioned him by the general superintendent six hours after he had delivered the California fruit special "on time."

The young railroader went at the missing pay car case just as he started at anything he undertook--with ardor and intelligence. He lined up all the facts in order, he met Adair down the line at Maddox, and Zeph Dallas was with him.

By three o'clock in the afternoon Ralph knew all there was to gather up as to the details of the missing pay car. It was not much to know. No trace of it had been found. There were a dozen theories as to what had become of it. Two of Adair's helpers favored one looking to the bold running off of the car after being detached by a "borrowed" engine of the Midland Central, and were working along that line.

Adair told Ralph that he was anxious to get after the five men with whom Zeph Dallas had been making friends for a week or more. Their leader was Rivers, and there was no doubt that this crowd had worked on the pay car robbery.

As Zeph had tearfully narrated to Ralph when he had implored his aid, the crowd had fooled him completely. From the start they must have had an inkling as to his identity. Working on that knowledge, as Zeph expressed it, they had simply "had fun with him."

The deceptive Rivers had left false telegrams purposely in Zeph's way. He had got up fictitious interviews with his confederates to which Zeph had listened, believing himself a shrewd eavesdropper.

They put up a plausible plan which diverted his investigations entirely from their real intentions, and this was how he never dreamed for a moment that they had the slightest hint as to the starting of the substitute pay car out of Rockton.

The day of that event they had sent Zeph on a fool errand to pretended accomplices at a desolate spot thirty miles from any railroad. Returning to the old camp of the conspirators the next morning foot sore and wearied, Zeph had found it utterly abandoned. The crowd had deserted him for good, and he was left "to hold the bag," as he ruefully expressed it.

There was "one great big thing" that Zeph had done, however, and Ralph encouragingly told him so. He had managed to get possession of papers and lists that gave the names and plans of the conspirators who were acting for the rival road, and also the cypher telegraphic code they used.

So valuable did Adair consider this information, that he declared it would not only result in proving where the real responsibility rested for the various loss and damage of late to the Great Northern, but he believed that when confronted with the proofs the Midland Central officials, rather than court legal proceedings would foot every dollar of the expensive bill run up by their spies, even to the pay car loss.

So, after telling Ralph that he should spend a day in consultation with the superintendent and others at Stanley Junction, and to advise him at once of any new discoveries of importance, the road officer left Ralph and Zeph hopefully to their own devices.

At exactly ten o'clock the next morning as the general superintendent and Adair sat in earnest consultation at headquarters. Glidden arrived in great haste with a telegram.

"A pink, sir," he reported to the head officer. "Was in cypher. From Fairbanks."

"Hello!" commented Adair, rising from his chair interested. "That's good. He never wastes electricity unless he has something to tell."

"Why," almost shouted the superintendent, roused up to tremendous excitement, "he has found the missing pay car!"

"He beats me, and that's fine, quick work!" declared Adair. "I told you he was a genius, and I knew what I was about when I sent for him."

"Listen to this," continued the superintendent hastily: "'Pay car found--north Eagle Pass. Smashed. Empty. Adair must come at once.'"

"I guess so," nodded the road detective with animation. "What a record: Roundhouse wiper, towerman, fireman, engineer, train dispatcher, and now beating the special road service right on its own grounds! Chief, where are you going to put Fairbanks next?"

"Something better and something soon," said the gratified superintendent. "He deserves the best."

"There's nothing better than chief dispatcher," declared old John Glidden, loyal to the core to the proud traditions of his calling. "You just keep Fairbanks right at my side--we're both happy and useful right here."

Adair waited for no regular train. A special locomotive took him down to Maddox, to find Ralph and Zeph awaiting him in a private room off the operator's office.

"Found the pay car, eh, Fairbanks?" challenged the road detective briskly.

"Yes, Mr. Adair--what was left of it."

"Knew you would, if anyone did. So I bungled? Well, I'm glad to learn what I don't know. Give us the details."

Ralph was brief and explicit. The first investigating party under Adair's direction had traversed all the southern cut offs. They had forgotten or neglected the one over which Ralph had made his sensational run with the California fruit special. It was no wonder that the division superintendent had considered it impossible, for at places the fruit special had ploughed up dirt and dead leaves matted down over the rails two feet thick.

At all events, recalling the obstruction of the chained ties, Ralph and Zeph had gone to the spot.

"That obstruction," explained Ralph, "had certainly been placed before the theft of the pay car, anticipatory of what was planned to happen."

"Yes, it looks that way," nodded Adair thoughtfully.

"The car must have run on strong gravity to the bumper, and went over the edge of the roadway at that point. She struck down over one hundred feet, breaking through the tops of trees. The snow later covered all traces of the descent. You will find the car lying near an old abandoned quarry house, a mere heap of kindling."

"And the safes and the money parrels?"

"Not a trace. However, Mr. Adair, it is no easy way to get out of the ravine with those stout heavy bank safes, and I advise that a guard be left in the vicinity."

"You have solved the mystery of the pay car, Fairbanks," said the road officer in a gratified tone--"now to find out what has become of the plunder."

"You will remain here, Mr. Adair?" inquired Ralph.

"Until I have made a thorough investigation and placed my men, certainly," responded the detective.

"I wish to put in a few hours at a side line investigation, if you please, and may not see you again until tomorrow, and I wish to take Dallas with me."

"All right," said Adair. He looked as if he would like to know more of Ralph's plans, but he had too much confidence in his young helper to question him.

As to Ralph, he had a decided reason for not explaining to the road officer. Glen Palmer was on his mind strongly, and a good many strange things that Glen had told him had impressed him with the conviction that the grandfather of the unfortunate Glen had been a pretty important element in the plots of the conspirators all along the line.

Zeph, while at the camp of the plotters, had heard considerable they did not intend him to hear. They had spoken of the Palmers--grandfather and grandson, many times.

"From what they said," declared Zeph, "I could easily decide that they discovered old Palmer, knowing him to be just the man they could use. Without Glen knowing it, they got him away from home several times. They played on his simple vanity, making him believe they would later get him a great job with a big railroad. Glen was heart-broken when he discovered this. The crowd finally got his grandfather in captivity. Glen tried to rescue him, and they caged him up, too."

"I begin to understand the circumstances under which the poor fellow sent those two warning messages," murmured Ralph. "Thief or no thief, he was loyal to me."

"I think it, too, and I think he could tell you lots," said Zeph. "I know his grandfather could. Both escaped finally, but where they went I don't know."

Ralph knew at least where Glen was. He remembered the town at which his arrest had been reported. It was less than twenty miles distant, and they caught a fast freight. Ralph went at once to the workhouse of the thriving little town. He inquired for Glen Palmer, but was informed that the following day was visitor's day, and that the rules were never broken except on special orders from the superintendent, who was absent at present.

"I will call tomorrow, then," said Ralph. "I wish, though, you would see Glen Palmer and tell him so. He may have some important message for me."

"You guessed it, sure enough," reported the prison guard, returning with a folded fragment of a note. "Young Palmer was frantic to know you was here, and says please don't forget and come tomorrow."

"I will certainly be here, or some one representing me," promised Ralph, and then he read the note, which ran:

"I am terribly anxious to know if my grandfather arrived safely at the home of my friend, Gregory Drum, at Ironton, where I sent him a few days ago."

Ralph and his companion went on to Ironton at once. They located the Drum residence, but did not find its proprietor at home. His wife, a thin, nervous lady, told how a few days before an old man named Palmer had come there, saying that his son was well known to her husband, which the lady believed to be true.

"He acted so strange I was nearly frightened to death," narrated the lady. "The second day here I found him astride of the roof ordering some imaginary men to string it with wires. The next day a neighbor came running in to tell me that he was up on a telegraph pole with a little pocket clicker. My husband was away, I was frightened for the man's good as well as my own, and I had him taken in charge by the town marshal. He'll treat him kindly till my husband returns, and Mr. Palmer will be in safe hands."

Ralph followed up this explanation by going at once to the marshal's headquarters. There was a low, one-story building with an office, and a barred room comfortably furnished beyond. The marshal listened to Ralph's story with interest.

"I'll be glad if you can make head or tail out of the old fellow," he said, and led the way into the barred room.

"Hello!" exclaimed Ralph, with a violent start as he entered the apartment.

"Thunder! I say, where did you get him?" ejaculated Zeph Dallas, with an amazed stare.

Across a cot lay a man asleep. He wore a stained bandage across his head and was haggard and wretched looking.

"Oh, that?" replied the marshal. "That's mystery No. 2. That's a bigger puzzle than the old telegrapher. He's the man we picked up mad as a March hare, with twenty thousand dollars in banknotes in his pockets."

"Zeph," spoke Ralph in a quick whisper, "you know who it is?"

"Sure, I know who it is," responded Zeph with alacrity. "It's Rivers, the king bee of the pay car robbers."

CHAPTER XXXI—QUICK WORK

The young train dispatcher had made a momentous discovery. He beckoned Zeph to follow him on tiptoe so they should not disturb nor be seen by Rivers. They somewhat surprised the marshal by crowding out of the room.

"There's the queer old fellow, Palmer, you asked about," said the official, pointing to a form occupied at a table at the other end of the room. "Don't you want to see him?"

"No, not just now," replied Ralph, drawing the man confidentially to one side. "We have not come here out of curiousity, but on a question of great importance. I represent the Great Northern Railroad, and you can help us very greatly."

"Can I? Good. I'll do it, then," instantly answered the marshal. "I'm not used to having such heavy cases as those two in there, and they pester me."

"Tell us about the man who seems hurt and sick."

"Why, he was brought in a few nights since by our man who watches the rivermen. They're a rough, bad lot. He found this man on a carouse in one of their haunts. Showing all kinds of money. He watched them, and jumped in just as they attacked the man and were about to rob him. We found over twenty thousand dollars in bank notes on the man--think of that! Only once since then has he entirely recovered from that cut on his head, and refused to give his name or say a word, except that his money came from a gold mine."

"Yes, a gold mine on wheels," observed Zeph pointedly.

"The man's mind is affected by the blow he got, and only a few minutes at a time has he been rational. He offered me all his money if I'd let him go. Funny thing, though; in one of his spells early this morning I found him whispering to old Palmer."

"Did you?" pressed Zeph eagerly.

"The old man ain't right, you know, but he sticks to that click-clack contrivance all the time. I watched the two, and the prisoner promised Palmer all kinds of things if he'd get free and send a certain message to a certain party, or somehow get the telegram sent. Well, since then the old man has been terribly busy with his play telegraph device, and excited, too. About an hour since he calls me to him, and says he will certainly get me a thousand dollars if I will take a message to the operator here. Only ten words, he says--one hundred dollars a word. I told him I wouldn't do anything until the sheriff came back tomorrow. He said only ten words. I asked him what ten words, and he shot out a lot of gibberish I couldn't take in."

"A cypher telegram," murmured Zeph.

"Well, I left it that way."

"Let me lurk around a bit, will you?" inquired Ralph.

"Certainly," assented the marshal.

For the next ten minutes Ralph, hidden in a corner of the detention room, posted himself and listened. When he came out his face was excited and eager.

"Don't let those prisoners send out a word or see a single person until I come back to you," he directed the marshal.

"All right. Found out something?"

"I think I have. I'll know for sure inside of six hours."

"And let me know, too. You see all this bothersome mystery is worrying me."

"You first of all," declared Ralph, "and you won't lose by coöperating with us."

"I see you're smart boys," observed the inexperienced marshal, "and I trust in your word to straighten out this tangle."

"What, Ralph?" broke in Zeph eagerly, as they left the place.

"I think I've got the clew."

"To what?"

"The whole pay car business--at least the start of one."

"Tell me about it."

"I simply listened to Glen's grandfather at his dummy ticker. Poor old man! He fancies he is being sought for by great railroad systems all over the world to take charge of their business. He ticked off all kinds of telegrams to important people. Then I caught the thread of a message he seemed to have particularly on his mind. It is just ten words, and of course must be the one he wanted the marshal to send. There it is."

Ralph showed a card on the back of which he had penciled down the following words:

"Rajah Sun and Moon Aeroplane Spectacles exemplar. Pardon Star Mudji."

Quick as a flash Zeph hauled out the written screed he had acquired while in the company of the conspirators. It comprised the formula of their cypher code.

"Advise Jem and Parsons," he translated at once. "Barn loft plunder. Get me bail." "Who to, Ralph?" he inquired eagerly--"the telegram."

"Mrs. Hannah Clifton, Dunbar Station."

"A relative, I'll bet. You're right, we've got the clew! 'Barn loft plunder.' Ralph, Dunbar Station, quick!"

"Yes," said the young dispatcher quietly, "that's our terminus, as quick as we can make it."

Ralph's special pass furnished him by the road officer came in good.

It brought them a lift on an urgency locomotive and another on the tender of the Daylight Express. At three o'clock that afternoon after due inquiry the two friends approached a house in a lonely settlement at the edge of Dunbar Station.

As they neared the house a woman knitting on its steps arose hurriedly, ran into the house and shut every door and window about the place.

"Acts sort of scared, eh?" suggested Zeph, as they approached the front of the house.

"Or suspicious," remarked Ralph.

"Stop right there. Who are you, and what do you want?"

The boys paused summarily, a bit taken off their balance. Very suddenly the barrel of a long shotgun was thrust through the slats of one of the wooden shutters, and the voice which challenged them showed no timidity or nonsense.

"We want to see Mrs. Hannah Clifton," replied Ralph politely, revealing himself.

"What for?" demanded the uncompromising invisible challenger.

"Why--er--that is--" began the rattled Zeph stammeringly.

"Shut up," whispered Ralph unceremoniously. "In behalf of Mr. Rivers," added Ralph ahead.

"He sent you, did he?"

"We just came from him."

"On business, I suppose?"

"Yes, madam."

"All right, then he gave you a word."

"Password!" whispered Zeph desperately.

"Sun and Moon," ventured Ralph recklessly.

"Wrong!" cried the woman as quick as lightning. "I see your game. You're guessing. If you don't make yourselves scarce in two minutes, I'll fire."

She did not wait the limit. The fowling piece scattered skithering bird shot with a flare just as the intruders got out of range.

"She's too keen for us--get to the barn, Ralph," suggested Zeph breathlessly.

"Yes, run," ordered Ralph.

They reached it, ran to cover and peered out. The woman, gun in hand, dashed from the house in the direction of a nest of small huts in the vicinity.

"She is going to rouse up some of her friends, I have not the least doubt," observed Ralph. "Quick action, Zeph. That telegram said 'barn loft!'"

"Whoo-oop!"

Already the impetuous Zeph had acted on the impulse of the moment. He was up in the loft already. Mingled with his chucklings were the rustlings of hay, a dragging sound. Down on Ralph's head came a bulky object as he started up the cleated side of the barn.

"Bags--two of them! Money! Pay envelopes!" gasped the young road officer in a transport of wild excitement. "Rivers hid them here. The woman don't know. Hustle, get out. She may bring a mob after us. Oh, I'm a--I'm a great detective at last!"

"You are, and always were," cheered Ralph with a happy smile. He felt well satisfied. The very feeling of the stuffed bags, a mere glance at their contents, told the young railroader that they were lugging to safety a fortune probably amounting to over two hundred thousand dollars.

They lost no time in cutting across the fields towards the town, each bearing a share of the precious burden.

At the local bank Ralph amazed the proprietor by demanding that the bags be locked up in his strongest vaults as the property of the Great Northern railroad.

Then he hurried to the office of the company railroad operator at Dunbar Station.

There was a brief explanation, a quick call for headquarters, the urgency signal, 25, and Ralph could fancy loyal old John Glidden at headquarters throwing open the entire lines for final orders in the great pay car mystery case.

East, west, south the messages flew: to the general superintendent, to Bob Adair, to the marshal, to the paymaster at Stanley Junction.

The unobtrusive station operator stared in bewilderment at the quick, natty stranger, who seemed to have no trouble in keeping track of a dozen different messages at once. It took Ralph fully an hour, with details, repeats and clean up. He arose from the instrument with a satisfied face.

"I've done my work, Zeph," he said, "and I'm going back to headquarters. You are to wait here for instructions from Mr. Adair. They will come sharp and brisk, don't be afraid. We have started the ball rolling, the rest will be easy."

CHAPTER XXXII—CONCLUSION

"What are you doing here, Fairbanks?"

Ralph had just entered the train dispatcher's office after a good night's sleep and sat down at his usual post of duty.

He felt pretty good, for he was rested up, and Glidden had spared a minute from some rush business to tell him that Adair had coralled the whole crowd of conspirators, bank bullion and all.

The general superintendent of the Great Northern, however, seemed to feel even better than Ralph himself. He had swung into the office with bright eyes and a beaming face, and while his challenge might sound to the uninitiated like a conventional call down, the head official looked as if he would like to grab the hand of his loyal, useful young assistant and hurrah at him.

"Getting back to routine, sir," said Ralph with a pleasant laugh.

"Wrong box."

"I'm afraid I don't quite understand," began Ralph.

"Don't. Then I'll show you," announced the official with a forcible chuckle. "Can't have insubordination and men out of place in this service. There's your desk," and seizing Ralph by the arm the superintendent led him past the counter into the little office rarely occupied, and marked on its door "Chief Dispatcher--Private."

"I will need your signature to get some autograph pads made," continued the official, picking up the stand containing the various rubber stamps in use. "What are you staring at, Fairbanks?"

"You don't mean--"

"Promotion? oh, yes, I do. That was settled on after the fruit special affair, but so many rushing things came along since we couldn't get around to you. Just make out a list of your new office requirements and changes in men and routine, and I'll O. K. them."

There was a suspicious sound in the open doorway. It was half between a sniffle and a chuckle.

"Here, you old rascal!" cried the superintendent, reaching out and grabbing the escaping Glidden, "no hanging around here," and he dragged him into the room. "First official act, Fairbanks, discharge this man. Then make him assistant manager. He's too fine for a simple first trick man."

"Oh, but you're doing things!" commented the old operator, trying to disguise his aroused emotions.

"For those who have done things for us, exactly," answered the superintendent briskly. "Both of you come to my office at 10 a. m. You will probably be interested in hearing the final wind-up of the pay car mystery."

It was certainly a remarkable meeting, that which the two friends attended.

Bob Adair was there with his report, brisk, animated and proud of his success. Zeph Dallas, excited and delighted, seemed to grow a foot when the superintendent gave him a personal word of praise for his efforts.

The initial work of Ralph Fairbanks had started in action all the efficient machinery of the road. As Zeph described it, once the first clew got to Adair he just seemed to spread out a great net and caught everybody and everything in it.

By midnight five of the principal conspirators had been run down and locked up. Some confessions were the result. Best of all, these brought out the secret connection of these men with the rival road.

"There is a pretty heavy bill to pay, but certain officials of the Midland Central will be glad to pay it," declared Adair.

"What had the robbers done with the bank bullion?" inquired the superintendent.

"They had no means of breaking open the strong safes quickly, and dropped them all down the well near the old deserted hut in Eagle Pass, intending to return later when the chase was over and rifle them at their leisure."

"Yes, that was the real gold mine Rivers boasted about," submitted Ralph.

"We have secured a list of all the 'suspicious' men among the telegraphers," continued Adair. "They will trouble us no further with delays, smash-ups and cut wires. Chief Dispatcher Fairbanks has already cleared the service, and the Great Northern can go on its way smoothly."

There was one favor Ralph asked before the conference broke up. This was that the fireman who had helped him in the record run of the California fruit special be remembered. It was granted, and the honest fellow was given a promotion.

"On the side, Fairbanks," said the road officer, familiarly linking Ralph's arm as they left the office of the general superintendent, "I wish to express a change of opinion on one subject."

"What is that, Mr. Adair?" inquired Ralph.

"Glen Palmer."

"You have seen him?" asked Ralph with interest.

"Yes, and you will see him, too, as soon as he is pardoned, which will be within twenty-four hours, if the influence of the Great Northern counts for anything. He is a noble young fellow."

"I thought that all along."

"I didn't, and I am ashamed of myself for the sentiment. He is no thief, and never was a thief."

"Not even--"

"The department store episode? No. He was trying to escape from the conspirators, who pressed him closely. He found himself stranded without a penny in an unfriendly town. In order to get the money to place his aged relative in a position of safety, he pretended to take the jewelry we know about so his grandfather could claim the ten dollars reward and carry out their plans."

"I am truly glad to hear this," said Ralph warmly. "And the convict portrait Ike Slump had?"

"Is really that of a cousin very much resembling Glen. He was the cause of Glen's wanderings and troubles. He was a sad scamp, but his health is broken. He escaped from jail, and Glen was willing to shoulder his identity until he got safely out of the country, where he now is trying to redeem his broken past."

"What of the old grandfather, Mr. Adair?"

"Glen wishes to repurchase the chicken farm. He loves the business. His grandfather is at heart a harmless old man, and Glen believes would soon forget his vagaries and settle down to a happy life."

"They shall have all the help I can give them," promised Ralph heartily.

Adair accompanied Ralph as far as the dispatcher's office. Glidden had preceded them. He just sat down at the operating table when a click at his instrument caused first trick man, second trick man, copy operator and Ralph himself to listen attentively.

A call had come giving a "sine" or signature that never ran over the wire without making every man in the dispatcher's office sit up and take notice-- the "sine" of the president of the Great Northern himself.

"For you, Mr. Fairbanks," spoke the old operator with a vast chuckle and excessive politeness: "Mr. Fairbanks, Chief Dispatcher Great Northern: Congratulations."

"Fairbanks," spoke the road officer, grasping the hand of the young railroader warmly, "I'm proud of you!"

Ralph flushed with pride and pleasure. But however warmly the generous words of commendation from the railroad men thrilled the young chief dispatcher, they paled into insignificance when the lad, on reaching home that night, heard his mother say:

"Ralph, my son, you have made me very proud!" And then, woman-like, she added: "But don't do it again, Ralph. You--you might get hurt!"

"All right, mother," he promised, as he kissed her. "Only I don't believe those chaps will have a chance to make trouble for me or the railroad again--that is, not right away."

THE END

Milton Keynes UK
Ingram Content Group UK Ltd.
UKHW020838260624
444769UK00011B/366